THE
PRINCE'S FAKE
FIANCÉE

DARCY FLYNN

ACKNOWLEDGEMENTS

Heartfelt thanks to my editor, Alicia Dean, for jumping on this project at the last minute. As always, your insightful critique has made my story better.

To my creative team, Rae Monet for her gorgeous cover design, Karen Duvall for creating the flat, and Jesse Gordon, my formatter. Thank you.

And to my beta reader, Brenda Jeffries, thank you for catching those pesky typos.

Jeanne Hardt, I so appreciate your critique and timely suggestions and most of all your wonderful friendship. And to Cindy Brannam for always being there for me.

To our 14-year-old former selves, and to all who believe that dreams really can come true.

CHAPTER 1

"Is this some kind of joke?" Prince Marcus de Blecourt of Sterlyn stood near the stone fireplace in the drawing room and gaped at his man, Percy.

"I'm very sorry, Your Highness, but this is the young lady the agency assigned to escort you while you are visiting the United States."

"And tell me again why you couldn't acquire the services of a young woman from a modeling agency?"

"This is a young woman, Your Highness."

"You know what I mean."

Percy cleared his throat. "The queen thought it best to hire someone from a security firm. Someone who'd already been vetted."

"Vetted?"

"For your safety, sir. After all, your coronation is less than two months away."

"I'm visiting New York City, not some wild, far-off jungle."

"Same difference, Your Highness."

The prince huffed a sigh. "What about the social events? My public appearances? I made it quite clear she was to be in attendance. How else is she to pose as my latest...interest?"

"Don't you mean betrothed?"

"One step at a time, Percy."

Marcus took one look at the woman's photo and plopped down in the Queen Anne chair near the hearth.

Percy peered over the prince's shoulder. "She is rather scary looking."

"She is indeed. No makeup, hair pulled tightly away from her stoic face. And that's a compliment."

With her old-fashioned bun, she reminded him of Nanny Jane. All this girl needed to complete the ensemble was Nanny's severe expression plus forty years of wrinkles, then she'd be formidable indeed. But he wasn't four anymore. He was thirty-four and had no need for a nanny or for protection from someone who reminded him of one.

The prince stood and began to pace. "No one will believe she's my latest or, most importantly, my fiancée. No offense to the young lady, but even the tabloids know where my taste in woman lie and frankly it's not her." He tossed the photo aside.

"And that's why we've taken steps to assure Your Highness that by the time you arrive in New York, she will be."

"And pray tell, what steps are those?"

"It's my understanding that her employer is taking care of those details."

The prince glanced again at the photo and found that promise highly unlikely. He was due to arrive in New York City in four days and looking at the woman's face and overall appearance, he imagined bringing her up to his standards in so short a time would take a minor miracle.

Irritated at the situation, he stepped back to the fireplace, snapped up an iron poker and jabbed the burning logs. As usual, this change of events had his mother's manipulating hands all over it. His patience was beginning to run thin and he had half a mind to stay in New York. The crown be damned.

He placed the poker back in its rack and glanced out the window. A light snow fell gently onto the well-manicured boxwoods in the garden below. Most years the first snow fell in December and this one was no exception.

The footman entered the drawing room. "Excuse me, sir. Lady Pricilla Rothschild is here to see you."

"Thank you, O'Brian."

Marcus glanced at Percy as the lady in question strolled in. Dressed in a cashmere coat and leather boots, she looked as if she'd stepped from the pages of the latest fashion magazine.

"Pricilla. What brings you to Sterlyn Castle?"

Lady Pricilla stepped forward and kissed his left cheek, then his right. As he dutifully accepted, he caught Percy's unmistakable frown.

After her skillful and semi-affectionate display, Pricilla turned toward Percy. "Please tell Minifred that we'll have tea in the atrium."

Percy, who took orders from no one except the royal family, looked toward him for his instructions. Marcus gave his man a decisive nod and Percy acknowledged with a slight bow from the hip, then left.

Pricilla looped her hand under the prince's arm and strolled beside him as they crossed the great hall.

"Once we're married that man will have to learn to take orders from me. I'm surprised you allow him to ignore my wishes the way you do."

"The key word being...if and when we're married."

They entered the high-ceilinged glass and metal framed conservatory. A comfortable seating area comprised of wicker furniture sat in the center of the room surrounded by an array of tropical plants, ferns and palms in stone planters of various sizes.

"I admit, ours would be a marriage of convenience. But don't you think it's time to stop fighting the inevitable?"

Yes, and why he'd spent his adult years single and would continue to do so for as long as he could. Seeing whomever he wished, whenever he wished it.

The thought of spending the rest of his life with Lady Pricilla Rothschild was more than he could bear. She'd claimed to have no love for him, only fondness. Maybe it was simply a foolish fairy tale, but he wanted love.

"Well, he has to start sometime, but until then..." She turned abruptly, wrapped her arms around his neck and settled her lips against his—as if staking her claim.

A few seconds later, he placed his hands on her arms and pulled, giving her no choice, but to release him.

"What is it, darling?"

"The cushions are damp. The staff must have watered recently. Let's go."

As Minifred entered the atrium, the prince informed her they would be having tea in the drawing room after all. She nodded and hurried back in the opposite direction. She'd just finished setting up the tea service when he and Pricilla entered.

"Thank you, Min," he said.

She bobbed a curtsy and left.

"The way you address your help as if they're your friends." Pricilla gave a well-practiced roll of her eyes and shook her head. "Your father is spinning in his grave."

"Which shows how little you know of my father. These people are my friends. And except for Min, I've known them all of my life."

He settled back on the damask covered chair and crossed his legs. Pricilla took the seat to his right, then poured the tea. After she'd filled each cup, she lifted a skillful hand, plucked up one sugar cube, then placed it with deliberate and well-practiced decorum into the royal embossed china.

In a seamless move, she crossed one shapely leg over the other as she brought the cup of tea to her glossy lips. No doubt, her carriage and manner were perfect...befitting a future princess. Heaven help him, he wanted more than outward perfection. So much more.

"Well done, Pricilla. Your graceful moves in serving tea play like a well-choreographed dance."

"Thank you, but you must know, your sarcastic comment won't deter me one little bit."

He lifted the teacup to his mouth.

This wasn't the first time Pricilla had used the M word in his presence. For years it had been understood the two of them would someday marry, but at thirty-four she was the last person he saw himself tied to for the rest of his royal life.

Considered a natural beauty by the press, Pricilla was indeed a lovely woman. No doubt about it with her carriage, her manner and her poise. But beauty was more than the outer appearance.

As prince, he'd had his share of escorting gorgeous women over the course of his adult life, and frankly, he'd grown tired of the outward preening and tedious decorum. Not to discount physical beauty, but the women he'd enjoyed most were the ladies who'd also displayed an inner beauty. The ones who'd been relaxed in his company and who didn't take themselves too seriously. In his estimation, kindness, thoughtfulness, and a generous spirit were also important qualities for basing a life-long commitment. Character traits which Pricilla sorely lacked.

He had no intention of marrying her, and the sooner he told her, the better for the both of them. He knew she'd expected it. Heck, his own mother expected it and, unfortunately for him, continued to plan for it.

The queen was a kind but formidable woman who ruled their small kingdom with grace and strength. There were expectations, and he'd hoped his attempts to delay finding a bride would allow time for his mother to see things differently.

If she only had his well-being at heart, he could understand her insistence he marry. But the fact that his coronation could not take place until he was married exasperated him. Making marriage nothing more than a means to an end. Love, unfortunately, had nothing to do with it.

As a young duchess, she'd married the man her father had chosen for her—King Maxwell de Blecourt of Sterlyn, and they'd lived many years with contentment and respect, but as nice as those two things were, they were not enough for him.

"Pricilla, you've made it quite clear you wish to marry me, to become the Princess of Sterlyn."

"Our parents planned this union since we were children. You know it and I know it. It's expected. Therefore, it is of little importance as to whether or not either of us wish it. It's time you accepted that."

"Is that the only reason?"

"Of course not. I want to marry you."

"Why?"

"I just told you."

"So, a marriage of convenience for everyone, except for us. Is that it?"

"Darling, we're perfect for each other. Besides, what's wrong with convenience?"

"Listen to what you're saying."

"You and I have been betrothed practically since birth," she said.

"An understanding between our families—hardly a betrothal. Do you even love me, or is it simply the idea of me that you love?"

"I'm very fond of you, Marcus, and I believe in time we could learn to love each other. But I have to admit, I do love the idea of us and the life that would entail."

"Well, at least you're honest about it."

"Oh, don't let it bother you so." She selected a sweet confection from the three-tiered server and placed it on her plate.

"Aren't you the least bit curious there might be someone else out there for you? Someone who'd be unexpected—a surprise. Someone in which to share true love?"

"True love is highly overrated. Companionship, respect—these are the things that make for a lasting relationship. Why look at your own parents—"

"I have and frankly that's what concerns me."

"I'm perfect for the job and everyone, but you, knows it," she said.

"If by everyone you mean parliament and my mother—"

"Look around you, darling. Who else would you choose?"

"If it only takes looks, one's position in society, and airs to make a princess, then I'm certain I could find an assortment of willing candidates for the position."

"You think so?"

"I do."

Pricilla gave a curt nod toward the woman in the photo. "Too bad you can't try it with her."

"How so?"

"Just look at her. She lacks all three."

"Maybe I should add cruel to the list, making it four." Even though he'd pretty much thought the same thing, it galled him to hear her say it.

"Speaking the truth is not cruel." She stood abruptly. "Look, don't make any decisions about us until after your trip to the United States."

"I'm sorry, Pricilla, but I—"

"I believe, after some time away, you'll find we're perfectly suited for each other."

"Perfectly suited. How romantic." He stood and stuffed his hands deep within his pockets. "I'm surprised at your insistence in the matter. Aren't you concerned I may find someone else while I'm gone?"

She glanced at the photo of the woman from the agency. "I doubt it." She chuckled softly. "Not with her at your side to scare them away."

"What are you talking about?"

"Nothing your mother and I haven't already taken care of."

"It was your idea to hire an escort from a security firm, wasn't it?"

She shrugged her slender shoulders, placed her teacup in its saucer, and stood. "Your mother thought it a grand idea. Your penchant for having a beautiful woman at your side at all events has led some in parliament to feel you're not serious about your duties as Sterlyn's future king. We felt for the sake of optics that it was time for you to show some restraint."

Anger flared in his gut. "Is that so?"

"Your mother—"

He lifted a hand. "Not another word." He strode across the room and rang for Percy.

A moment later, his man appeared in the salon.

"Please see Lady Pricilla out."

With an appreciative gleam in his eye, Percy gave a slight nod, then stood aside for Pricilla to join him.

"Trust me, Marcus. Your mother and I are right about this. You'll see," she said.

Once they left, Marcus picked up the photo from the New York City security firm and gazed into the unsmiling face of the woman staring back at him. Even from the black and white photograph, her gaze assessed and analyzed, even to the point of passing judgment. Making him feel like it was *he* who was under her scrutiny—her evaluation and not the other way around. For the first time since he'd gotten the picture, he studied her features in more detail.

He imagined the severe mousy-brown hair style replaced with long, soft waves framing her oval face. He glanced at the gray jacket and white collared shirt, and although boring and unflattering, the corporate state of dress accentuated the hollow of her slender neck and throat. When his gaze finally settled on her full lips, he imagined a sheen of color there. If his staff could pull off her transformation it would be a miracle indeed.

For one second she stared right through him leaving him with the uncanny feeling that if he met her in person, she'd not hesitate to give him look for look. He knew instinctively this woman would not smile coyly to gain his attention nor flutter her eye lids one little bit.

Even though she didn't have Pricilla's natural beauty, there was something about her that fascinated him. Her defiant stare tossed a challenge. As if daring him in some way. He had to admit the temptation to take it lingered as he mulled over his situation.

He dropped the photo with the file on the low embossed walnut table at his knees. He was fully aware of his mother's concerns regarding what she referred to as his irresponsible actions and the optics they caused in regard to the monarchy. The prince took no joy in disrupting her plans for his future, but if she insisted on Pricilla being a part of those plans, then disrupt, he would.

As he stared back at the face of the woman in the photo, a plan of his own formed in his mind. In that moment, he knew he'd give her an audience, deferring to his mother's wishes, but it would be the last time.

* * *

Samantha Keller slapped the assignment papers with the back of her hand and stared angrily at her boss. "Is this a joke?"

"Sir," he said.

She licked her lips and swallowed. "Sir?"

Blake St. John folded his arms with a glare that told her to watch her step. As head of Colfax Security, he insisted all of his subordinates address him as Sir or Chief.

"No. It's not," he said. "You're assigned to the prince while he's in the city for his two-week visit. It was a last-minute thing."

"Why not send Beth Ann?"

"She's already assigned to another project."

"And Carmon?"

"Also busy."

"Oh."

"And, whether or not the assignment suits you is of no importance to me." He took his seat behind the large walnut desk. "It's a job and you'll do it."

"Excuse me, sir. When I signed up with Colfax, it wasn't to babysit some arrogant, royal pain in the—"

"May I remind you, Miss Keller, you're on probation with this firm. Drug tests don't lie. With your record at NYPD you should be thanking me you even have a job. And if you want to keep it, you'll follow my orders. Is that clear?"

"Yes, sir." She sucked in a breath and pushed back the painful memory.

"You haven't even met the man, so how do you know he's arrogant?"

"Magazines. The newspapers."

"You and your tabloids." He shook his head. "They're not reputable and you know it."

"Sir?"

"I've been in your cubical. Stacks of them."

She folded her arms and gave him her most stubborn—I couldn't care less what you think of my choice in reading material—stance.

"I don't understand you, Keller. Do you have any idea how many women would love to be in your shoes right now?"

"No, but I'm more than happy for one of them to

take my place. What about some of the other women who work here?"

"Believe me, if they would've accepted anyone else, I'd have gladly made the change."

"What do you mean?"

"I sent them all the available women for the job, and they chose you."

She unfolded her arms and shuffled from one foot to the other. "On my merits, right?"

He ran a skeptical gaze over her masculine, gray suit, cleared his throat, and rearranged some papers on his desk. "What other reason would there be?"

"Why not send one of the men?"

"A female was requested. *You* were requested." He handed her a card. "Here's your contact at The Carlyle Hotel. Apparently, you're also to accompany the prince to several functions while he's in New York."

"Wouldn't he have brought his own security detail with him?"

"I didn't ask," the chief said as he flicked his gaze from her severe bun to her sensible shoes. "They also requested I give you these." He handed her a stack of magazines. "They should help you prepare for your assignment. And, for heaven's sake, buy a dress."

She glanced down at her suit, then back at him.

"You're dismissed."

Once outside his office, Sam took a closer look at

the publications. "Fashion magazines?" *Vogue, Elle* and *Allure,* as well as a few she'd never heard of. The gorgeous cover models stared mockingly up at her from their glossy pages.

Job security or not, she had half a mind to march back into Blake's office and turn the job down, but dismissed that idea as soon as she'd thought it. She'd messed up big time as a rookie cop and no matter how much she hated the thought of shadowing some high and mighty prince, she'd just have to suck it up and do it.

Back in her cubical she dropped the magazines on the desk and sat down. She picked up her stash of celebrity tabloids, and rummaged through them until she found the one about the prince's upcoming visit. He was on the cover and looking all kinds of gorgeous in his regal attire.

She took note of his square jaw, his dark hair and brown eyes. She'd practically memorized the photo since she'd gotten it. He hadn't changed much from the teenager in the poster that once hung in her attic bedroom. He'd matured all right. And by his looks, every bit a prince.

She re-read the article, shaking her head at his playboy antics. Leaving hotel suites in shambles—all-nighters—bar brawls—

She'd have to remember to pack her pistol.

CHAPTER 2

Four days later, Samantha arrived at The Carlyle Hotel on the upper east side hauling a small suitcase behind her. According to the information the chief had given her, she would be staying at the hotel for the two weeks, all expenses paid by the royal family.

She paused outside the grand entrance, ran her gaze over the tall, narrow exterior, then pushed through the glass turn-style doors. As she approached the front desk, she took note of the time on the wall clock behind the attendant. She was early.

The man behind the counter lifted his gaze with a smile that suddenly vanished when he set eyes on her. "I'm sorry, but we're not accepting any applications for housekeeping at this time."

She flipped open her credentials and held them up to his face.

"I do apologize. Checking in?"

"No, I mean, I'm not sure." She slipped her security badge back into her inside jacket pocket. "I believe someone has acquired a room for me and may have already checked me in."

"Your name?"

"Samantha Keller. Mr. Neville Percy is expecting me. He may have been the one to make the reservation."

"Of course. Please have a seat, and I'll let him know you're here."

She walked to the nearest chair then lowered herself to the soft cushion. Folding her arms, she propped her leather sole shoes on the glossy low table at her feet.

As she glanced around the elegantly decorated lobby, she caught the attendant's disapproving eye. Realizing her mistake, she slowly removed her feet from the table and clasped her hands together in her lap.

A few minutes later, the attendant approached her.

"Miss Keller, Mr. Percy would like for you to go on up to our royal suite, floor 22."

"Thanks." She left the grand foyer, wondering who this Percy guy was and if the prince would also be there. As she entered the elevator she caught her reflection on the brass interior wall. She'd dressed in her usual gray suit, but instead of her white blouse, she'd chosen a light pink one instead. It certainly wasn't *Vogue* standards, but the best she could do on such short notice. The clothes in the fashion magazines were way too outlandish for her tastes, anyway.

On the ride up she thought about all those glamorous women splashed throughout the glossy pages of those magazines. Her days of trying to be like them were long past. And at twenty-eight, she had no intention of making the slightest effort to be, not even for royalty. She was here to protect the prince, not for fashion week. If the royal family didn't like it, then they could find someone else to protect him. As such, she would not be comfortable doing so in some classy outfit.

The royal suite stood several yards to the left of the elevator. In a few short strides, she faced the entrance and knocked. Seconds later, the door opened to a tall man dressed in a navy suit. His pleasant smile faded slightly when he set eyes on her. "Miss Keller?"

"At your service."

"Please, this way." He stepped back for her to enter.

She walked in, taking note of her surroundings.

"You can leave your suitcase by the door. I will show you to your room shortly."

"Thanks." She set the case to the side and followed him across the open space to a plush seating area. A Christmas tree decorated in silver and gold, stood in front of the full length arch window overlooking City Park.

She'd never been in such a swanky place before and wondered if they were all this large and beautifully furnished. With its high ceilings and what looked to be original art, this looked more like someone's upper east side brownstone, than a hotel suite.

She sat and for a brief moment, Percy stood, staring, as if he hadn't the slightest clue what to do with her. He finally took a seat opposite.

"Tea?"

"Sure."

It didn't take the brightest bulb in the room to know she'd caught the man off his guard.

"Excuse me for staring, but the prince and I were led to believe you'd co-operate with our request?"

"Request?"

"Your employer assured us he'd see to it."

"I'm sorry, but I'm not following."

"Your attire. Your state of dress." He glanced at her head. "Your...hair."

"Um..." She lifted her hand to her severe bun. "He supplied me with fashion magazines and told me to buy a dress. Aside from that..." She shrugged.

"They were to act as a guide as to what we expected from you during the two weeks in our employ. We assumed you'd dress accordingly."

"Sorry, but I don't own clothes like those depicted in the magazines. And since I took the job only a few days ago I hadn't any time to shop. But, even if I had, I couldn't afford such...finery."

"I see. Did your employer not tell you we'd be reimbursing you for any and all expenses incurred?"

"I'm sorry, but no, he didn't. Besides, even if he had, my credit cards have a limit."

"I see."

"Look, for what it's worth, it's obvious you've made a mistake in hiring me."

"I beg your pardon?"

"I can see the disappointment in your eyes." She ran her hand over her torso, "I'm afraid, all that high-end, *Vogue* stuff is just not me."

Percy ran his wide-eyed gaze over her masculine-cut, gray suit with all the abhorrence of the upper echelon of society. Good. Maybe he'd fire her and call another security agency to babysit the prince.

"It's okay, really. I understand if you'd like to find someone else."

"I'm afraid that's His Highness's prerogative."

"Oh." She picked up her teacup and eyed the finger sandwiches. "May I?"

"Of course."

"So," she took a bite, "when do you expect the prince?"

"Any moment now."

And on those exact words Prince Marcus de Blecourt of Sterlyn pushed open a set of adjoining doors
in the suite.

As if on cue.

As if all had been perfectly timed.

Oh gosh. There he is.

Sam paused mid-chew and watched the man approach. He was everything a prince should be. All
fairy tale wonderful. Tall, dark-haired, and extremely
handsome. Not even the tabloids had captured his
masculine good looks and regal air. And he looked absolutely nothing like the teenager from the frayed
poster that hung in her bedroom.

As he crossed the wool carpet, his gaze never left
her face, drawing her in with his warm, hypnotic
stare. He stopped in front of her, breaking the spell.

She blinked and came back to the present, realizing
there had to be a but somewhere. No one looked this
fine and smiled this beautifully with eyes the color of
autumn without a *but* attached.

"Your Highness. May I introduce Miss Samantha
Keller. Miss Keller, His Royal Highness, Marcus de
Blecourt of Sterlyn."

Sam shot to her feet and swallowed. She had no
idea if she were to curtsey or stick out her hand. But
Mr. Charming answered that question for her, when

he offered his. After a brief hesitation she took it and gave a half-hearted shake.

"Nanny Jane." He spoke softly.

"Um, what?"

His lips quirked a half-smile, and he gave a brief shake of his gorgeous head. "It's a pleasure to meet you, Miss Keller." The prince tilted his head ever so slightly.

"Please, call me Sam."

"I prefer, Samantha. If that's all right with you."

"Um, yeah, sure."

"The tea and cakes to your liking?"

"I haven't had the cake yet, but the tea is delicious."

"Please sit."

"Miss Keller is of the opinion that we should find a replacement for her." Percy poured the prince a cup of tea, then calmly positioned himself across the room.

The prince looked candidly at Sam. "Why is that?"

"Because you're expecting me to be something I'm not." She laughed nervously and wanted to kick herself for it.

"On the contrary, with a bit of make-up and the right clothes, you'll do just fine."

She blinked. "What do you mean, I'll do? Look, I'm here to protect you and my clothes have nothing to do with how well I do my job."

"Protect me?" He laughed. "I have legions protecting me. No, what I need is a companion while I'm here. An escort."

"Now, hold on a minute. That's not what I—"

"Not that kind of escort. Trust me," he flicked his gaze over her gray-suited figure, "no sexual favors will be required of you."

Her jaw dropped, as did her teacup, but the prince's quick action kept it from hitting the carpet.

She watched in horror as Percy jumped in to clean up the spilled liquid.

Without missing a beat, the prince said, "It is my custom to have someone accompany me to the various social functions I'm scheduled to attend while visiting abroad."

"I've done my research, Your Highness. And I'm well aware of the type of women you usually have at your side."

He sat back and folded his arms. A flicker of amusement in his eyes.

"That said, I think there's been a misunderstanding. I'm a security officer. I'm hired to protect people, not be their date."

He pinned her with his gorgeous stare. "Are you saying you don't want the job or that you're not up to it?"

"If you must know...both. With all due respect, I'm not the partying type. I'm an ugly duckling, and you want a swan."

His gaze softened. "And yet the ugly duckling turned out to be a swan, don't forget. She only thought she was a duck."

"Quack, quack. Trust me. I'm a duck."

He tilted his regal head to the side. "Who's told you such nonsense? Someone from your past?"

She lifted her chin. "My past has nothing to do with the here and now."

"If you say so." He regarded her with amusement.

She sucked in a deep breath. "I pretty much know who I am, and believe me, it's no swan. What you see is the real me. Not Miss *Vogue*." She didn't know why she felt the need to press the point, but it was important she not only establish but manage their expectations right from the beginning.

He flicked his gaze over her. "I disagree."

"That's a very nice thing to hear, and quite flattering, but—"

"You think I'm complimenting you to further my own interests?"

"That's not what I meant."

"Then you'll do it?"

The prince didn't know it, but she had no choice, but to do it. That is if she wanted to keep her job.

"May I ask why? I mean, you must have hordes of female companions who'd like nothing better than to promenade all over the city with you. Socialites, movie stars—"

"Yes, and with their sights on one thing."

"Don't tell me—to be the next Princess of Sterlyn."

"Your astuteness amazes."

"So, in a way, I am protecting you."

"Exactly."

She pressed her lips together. "Okay. I'll do it, but on one condition."

"Which is?"

"I choose what clothes to wear."

"That's fine as long as they're from the royal dresser."

"Royal dresser?"

"Yes. The royal dresser is a person. She'll have a variety of clothing for you to choose from. Most importantly, items that will be appropriate for each occasion in which you'll be accompanying me. You'll find the selection in the adjoining suite."

Suddenly overwhelmed, all Sam could do was nod.

He eyed the half-eaten sandwich in her hand. "You'll also need some instruction on decorum, proper manners."

"Excuse me?"

He answered her with the simple raising of his royal brow. She pressed her lips together and carefully placed the half-eaten sandwich back on her plate.

"And who's going to give me these most important lessons?"

"I am. Of course."

* * *

"You?"

"Yes."

"Listen, I'll be the first to admit that I don't know all the ins and outs of how high society, much less, royalty gets on. That said, I'm sure the royal dresser can give me all the pointers I'll need."

He eyed her severe hairdo and colorless outfit. "Sadly, your transformation will take more than a few pointers."

"I beg your pardon."

"No need."

Sam opened her mouth. The prince waited for her speak but, apparently, when no cutting remark came to mind, she clamped it shut. His intent had not been to insult her, but by her reaction, he most certainly had done so.

"Of course, if my mother were here, she would be the one to instruct you, but since she's not, and I'm the only royal present, the delightful burden falls to me."

"If it's such a burden—"

"Now, sit up. Back straight."

She lifted her chin and gave him a challenging look. "I'm sorry, but I'm not here to attend some...royal charm school. And for your information, I'm sitting just fine. I actually like the way I sit." She shot to her feet. "And, I like the way I stand." She swiveled, marched to the entrance and jerked up her suitcase handle. "I also like the way I walk out of here. Good day, your—your haughtiness."

In a flash, she disappeared through the door, slamming it shut.

Percy calmly stepped over to the prince. "So, what do you think?"

"Well. She's highly opinionated, spoke her mind, and cared not one whit for my position. Furthermore, she made no attempt to curtsy." The prince folded his arms and continued to eye the closed door. "She's perfect."

"Begging your pardon, sir, but I don't believe the young lady understands her actual role in the matter and I feel I must point out this is not at all what the queen had in mind when she secured Miss Keller's services."

"Making my effort to avoid marriage with Lady Priscilla Rothschild all the more entertaining."

* * *

Sam stood at the foot of the chief's desk as he questioned her.

"And after you insulted him?"

"I walked out."

He shook his head. "We need this account, Sam. Having the prince as our client will do wonders for our business. Someone of his caliber could open the door to other celebrities and political figures."

"I understand that, chief, but I believe I should at least have had a say in the matter. If you'd been there, then—"

"You can certainly turn down the assignment, but if that's your choice, then mine will be to fire you. So. Decide. But before you do, there's someone here who'd like to explain why you're needed." The chief pressed the intercom. "Kathy, send him in."

Sam glanced over her shoulder as the door to the office opened. Prince Marcus entered and strode with princely confidence across the small room. Sam folded her arms, glanced at the chief, then back at the prince.

"Miss Keller." The prince bowed slightly. "Ready for battle, I see."

"Your highness," Blake said. "Please take a seat."

"Please, call me Marcus."

The prince sat down and shifted his gaze to hers. His brown eyes held a hint of suppressed humor she found utterly annoying.

After a brief hesitation, she slowly took the seat next to him.

"I felt terrible how we left things yesterday," he said. "After your hasty departure, I realized I hadn't explained the situation very well. I want you and Mr. St. John to know that I take full responsibility as to how our meeting played out."

"Thank you, Marcus. And please, call me Blake."

Prince Marcus turned to Sam. "I apologize if I insulted you. Rest assured, that was never my intention."

"If?" She raised a brow.

"I apologize *for* insulting you."

"Like when you laughed when I told you my job was to protect you."

"Yes."

"And when you insulted my posture and eating habits?"

"That, too. Please accept my sincere apology."

When he tipped his head, she caught the humorous twinkle in his gorgeous eyes and wondered if there was a penalty for punching a visiting prince in the nose.

"As we discussed yesterday, you'll be part of my protection—my security team, but since you'll accompany me to all of the social functions, I'd like to keep your position a secret. You'll be incognito. I don't like to draw attention to the fact that I've hired another bodyguard, as I already have several. The media has enough ammunition against me as it is."

"Well maybe if you'd curb your bar brawls and playboy antics—"

"Keller!" The chief exploded from behind his desk. His appalled expression gave her pause.

"Please," Marcus said. "Miss Keller is right. In the past I have acted foolishly but hope to make amends to those I've affronted during my stay in New York." He turned a bland look in her direction.

"I still don't see why you need me?"

"I believe I made that clear to you, yesterday. You'll be the surprise element. The fly in someone's ointment, as you Americans like to say."

"We haven't said that in years and those who do are well over fifty."

"Keller." Although calmer now, the chief's tone of voice still held a sharp warning.

"Fine. I'll be your fly in the ointment."

"Excellent," the prince said.

As he took her hand, she was overcome with the urge to pull out right then and there. Job security or not.

"We'll continue your royal charm school lessons in the morning." When he leveled his Prince Charming smile at her, she could've sworn it said, *I win.*

CHAPTER 3

The following morning, Sam grabbed a quick breakfast from the old but functional kitchen in her family's Richmond Hill Victorian home, but before she could head out, her stepmother, Katherine, lifted her cheek for a kiss. As usual, her Step was all show and not much substance. Sam had gotten used to it over the years and dutifully complied.

"Keep your fingers crossed," Katherine said. "Tiffany is on Jason Osborne's yacht this coming weekend."

"The man's twice her age."

"And enormously wealthy," she said. "And capable of keeping my precious daughter in the life she's grown accustomed to. Or, so she says."

And while Tiffany spent her years growing accustomed, Sam and her stepmother did without. Sam's father was nothing if not fair, his will stating his daughter and stepdaughter would share equally in the estate after Katherine's death. But would there be anything left was the question. Good thing Samantha loved her job. Protecting others was her thing.

Once outside, she stopped at the iron gate and glanced over her shoulder at the old Victorian house. She'd hung a large Fraser Fur wreath with a crimson bow on the massive oak door, then topped off the greenery with several strands of multi-colored lights, framing the entrance like a giant Christmas card. It wasn't much, but beautiful in its simplicity.

She'd developed the habit of looking back at the house when she left for the day, as she had no idea if this would be the day the creditors would come calling and the day they'd all have to move out.

Another reason she could not lose her job. Three generations of Kellers had lived here, and now, if things didn't change, she'd be the last one. As much as it pained her, she still had a lifetime of wonderful memories with her father, and that would have to be enough.

Two hours later, Sam stood in front of the full-length mirror in her room at The Carlyle. The sky-blue dress felt like silk between her fingers and was the finest thing she'd ever seen, much less, worn. It fit her beautifully and for a moment all she could do was stare at her reflection. She ran her hands carefully over the bodice, stopping at her waist. Hands on hips she turned right, then left.

Eliza, the royal dresser, stood off to Sam's right, beaming. "That dress is lovely on you, miss. The prince has marvelous taste."

"The prince? I thought you chose this dress."

"No. He did."

"I see."

"Complements your light brown hair and fair skin."

"I don't even look like me."

Eliza smiled and winked. "I believe that's the point." Her eyes widened. "Oh pardon, miss. I didn't mean that the way it sounded."

Sam shook her head. "No offense taken." She frowned at her reflection. "But this'll take some getting used to." She turned away from the mirror and headed for the connecting door between her room and the rest of the royal suite.

"Miss Samantha, your shoes."

Sam paused and glanced at her feet—still snug in her black leather lace-ups. "Fine." She bent over and pulled one off, then the other. "But I can't walk in those." She pointed to the four-inch heels in Eliza's hands. "Don't you have anything I can actually wear without falling over?"

Eliza snatched up a pair of strappy sandals. "What about these?"

They were only about an inch shorter than the high heels.

"They'll have to do, I guess."

"We'll work on the spiked heels. I promise, with practice, you'll be able to manage."

"I hope so." She slipped on the sandals, straightened up, and left.

* * *

Marcus stood from the sofa when Samantha entered the room. Their eyes met, and she paused. After a brief hesitation, she stepped forward.

"Samantha. You look lovely."

"Thanks."

"That dress fits you perfectly."

"And how did you know it would?"

"I have an eye for these things."

"I bet you do."

Marcus waved her over to the small table for two. "Please have a seat."

She strode across the carpet.

"Stop," he said.

She stopped mid-stride and stared back with a blank expression.

"Let's try that again."

"Try what?"

"Walking."

Her lips pressed into a thin line, and her eyes narrowed. For a second, he thought she might explode.

"And just what is wrong with the way I walk?"

"You marched. You stomped. You're angry and it shows. Your display of aggressive behavior is quite unladylike." He pointed back to where she first entered the room. "Shall we try again?"

She spun in her strappy heels and stumbled forward. Marcus jumped to her side, catching her before she hit the carpet.

He gazed down at her as he cradled her in his arms. Her soft curves were evident as he held her against his chest. He took note of the glossy rose hue covering her parted lips. She drew in a long, slow breath as she gazed up at him, all vulnerable and sweet. She blinked, breaking the spell, and lowered her gaze as if fighting off her own attraction to him.

"Let me go." She spoke through clenched teeth.

Marcus made a point of eyeing the floor mere feet beneath her. "Right now? This very second?" He shot another quick glance at the floor and smothered a grin. "The way I see it, you should be thanking me."

Her chest heaved. She sucked in a breath. "Thank you."

He carefully set her upright. "Are you all right?"

"Yes. It's these blasted shoes. I'll never be able to walk in them by tomorrow night."

"Wait here."

A minute later, he returned from her room carrying a pair of white, low-heeled pumps.

"Slip these on."

She leaned forward and grabbed the heel of the left sandal. When she pulled down, she teetered right, nearly falling again. In one lithe movement, Marcus picked her up and carried her across the room.

Once she was seated, he knelt before her and slipped off one strappy heel, then the other. That done, he held the pumps at her feet. When she hadn't lifted either foot, he glanced up at her. She stared down at him, wide-eyed and unblinking.

"Cinderella?"

"Huh?"

He eyed the shoes. "Your slippers await," he couldn't resist saying and had the pleasure of seeing her cheeks flush the prettiest pink. She stammered something unintelligible and slipped her feet into the shoes.

"Shall we try this again?"

She gave a curt nod and strode across the room, her scowl plainly evident when she turned to face him.

He folded his arms. "Pretend you're at least a little happy to be here."

She squared her shoulders, took one step forward, then stopped. Scrunching her eyes tightly together, she shook her head, then lifted the long skirt up the right side of her leg.

Fascinated, he watched as she unstrapped the pistol and holster from her thigh, then set both aside.

Straightening up, she stepped slowly across the floor, stopping at the chair he held out for her. For a brief moment, their gazes locked, breaking only when he nodded toward the seat.

She sat, then lifted her body a fraction as he pushed her chair forward. He stepped around the table and took the seat opposite.

"That was much better," he said.

"Thanks to the lower heels."

"Now. Would you please pour the tea?"

After a brief hesitation, she picked up the delicate teapot with one hand while placing the tea strainer onto his cup with her other. She filled his cup, then hers.

"Very good. One might think you'd been practicing," he said with a lazy smile.

She lifted the teacup to her lips, glared at him from across the rim as she took a sip, then set the cup in its saucer.

"Is all of this extreme etiquette really necessary? I thought I was to accompany you to some social gatherings while you're in the city, but you act like I'm to be paraded before the queen."

"Yes, well... That's highly unlikely."

"But it so happens, I've had years of experience serving tea," she continued. "That said, I have been practicing and I hope my efforts have shown you I can manage quite well from here on out. What I do need from you, though, is your daily schedule."

He set his cup down and sat back. "I'll see to it that Percy gives you the itinerary. As to this other...the repetition is only necessary in order to make you comfortable. The more you practice, the more at ease you'll be in the public eye. Believe me, they can be quite ruthless when they want to be. Their constant scrutiny is as bad, if not worse, than the press."

"Which you, no doubt, know from experience," she said.

"I do. As you aptly pointed out in St. John's office yesterday."

"Well, you can rest easy Prince Marcus, I know how to deal with mean-spirited people."

"Which you feel qualifies you to handle the international press."

"Look." She sighed. "If you'd just be satisfied with me being me, I'll wear the expensive clothes and learn to walk in those blasted heels."

"It'll take more than that, I'm afraid. Your attitude—"

"I know how to be friendly. I know how to respect others."

"Yet your actions suggest otherwise."

A wave of doubt filled her lovely eyes as she struggled for a response.

He propped his chin in his hands and eyed her from across the table. "I get the impression that you have something against me."

Sam shifted uncomfortably in her seat. "Why would you say such a thing? I hardly even know you."

"My point exactly. If, as you say you hardly know me, then why the open hostility?"

"I didn't realize it was open. I'll have to watch myself."

"You see? There it is again. You *do* have something against me."

She lifted her chin. "I'd prefer not to answer that question. The verdict is still out, as they say."

He sat back, brown eyes brimming with humor. "And who, pray tell, are *they*? And where do *they* get such immense authority?"

Her chest heaved, and she bit her lower lip. "Prince Marcus, if you insist on continuing this nonsensical conversation, then I suggest you find someone else to escort you while in New York."

"Nothing nonsensical about it. You, my dear Miss Keller, are the first person to treat me with such open disdain."

"I... I apologize."

"No apology necessary. From the first moment when you stormed out of the suite, I found your disrespect quite...intriguing. I admire the fire in your belly, just be careful how you use it and to whom that fire is directed.

"I suggest you take the afternoon off for a time of... reflection." A small smile tugged at the corners of his mouth.

"If you must know," she said. "It's the packaging I resent and the fact that you assume one's appearance dictates one's manners. That said, I can get by all of that if you'd—"

"Let you, be you?"

"Exactly."

He gave a slight nod. "I can live with that as long as you're certain you can."

She dropped her gaze and touched the base of her neck. Seconds ticked by before she finally raised her eyes to his. "I can." She gave a curt nod.

"Now that's settled... Would you like a cake?" He secured a petit four with a pair of silver tongs. "It'd be a shame to let such a delicacy go to waste."

Her rosy lips quirked into a half smile. "I agree."

Samantha Keller was an extremely attractive woman and yet someone in her past had led her to believe just the opposite. To be honest, he'd missed it, as well. But in his defense, a black and white photograph was not the same as meeting her in the flesh.

His initial plan had been to use her to thwart Pricilla, and he still would, but he couldn't deny the growing desire to help her gain confidence in her own beauty. After all, he considered himself an expert when it came to beautiful women.

Hers was a rare, unusual, and most unique beauty. As if she'd held a hundred mysteries beneath her cool, sarcastic, no nonsense exterior. Samantha was indeed a swan. She just didn't know it yet.

Chapter 4

Sam sat at the 1920's walnut vanity table that had belonged to her mother and pulled open the small left-hand drawer. An assortment of lipsticks and a smattering of eye makeup filled the narrow opening. Some were hand-me-downs from Tiffany after she'd tired of the colors, claiming they were out of fashion. But they still looked perfectly fine to Sam.

As she fingered the small supply, she thought about her earlier conversation with the prince. Even though he'd put her in her place, she'd caught the unmistakable humor in his eye as he'd told her to take the afternoon to reflect.

The prince seemed to delight in toying with her. Admittedly, she'd deserved it. She hadn't hidden her disdain, as he'd called it. It was unlike her to be so openly rude and wrong of her to dishonor him. Smug or not, he didn't deserve that. But he was mistaken about one thing. Her attitude toward him. It wasn't rooted in dislike...or even disdain...but disappointment in who he'd become.

She continued to search the drawer and finally settled on a gold tube. Lifting it overhead she read the underside—Wild Rose Pink. She pulled off the cap and turned the bottom until the bright color appeared.

With a gentle stroke she applied the color to her upper lip. Just as she ran the color across the lower, her stepsister appeared at the door.

"I haven't seen you apply lipstick since middle school," Tiffany said. "So. Who is he?"

"Who's who?" Sam pressed her lips together sealing the color.

"The guy you're getting all glossy-lipped for."

Sam turned to find her smirky-mouthed stepsister leaning against the door jamb.

"Who says there has to be a guy? You, who never, ever, leaves this house without makeup on."

"That's because I never know who I might meet. Whereas you, well...you know," she shrugged, "have never been interested in your looks."

"A girl can change." She pulled out the eye wand from the mascara tube to find it completely dry.

Tiffany reached into her sparkly clutch, pushed away from the door frame, and handed her a long black tube. "Take mine."

"Where are you going?" Sam asked. "You're not eating with us?"

"Nope."

"This is the third night this week you haven't eaten with your mother." She shook her head and drew out the wand from Tiffany's mascara. "You shouldn't leave her like you do. Especially in her condition."

"She hasn't lost her mind yet, but what about you... missing from action the past two nights yourself."

"That's different. I'm working," she said, while carefully applying mascara to her left eyelash. "Speaking of which, I need you to stay with Katherine for the next two weeks or so while I'm on this new job. She shouldn't be left alone at night." She plunged the wand back in the tube, screwed the cap in place, then handed it back to Tiff.

"Fine, but I'm working too, don't forget."

"Schmoozing it up with the elite on some millionaire's yacht is not working."

"It is if I'm to snare a wealthy husband." She unsnapped her purse and slid the back tube back inside. "And when I do the three of us can live in style instead of this old heap."

"It's not a heap."

"Fine then. Your family home. Call it whatever you want, but it's still crumbling around our ears."

THE PRINCE'S FAKE FIANCÉE · 53

"This house is on the historic registry and has only started crumbling since you and Katherine have spent practically everything my father left us."

"Always whining. Mother has just acquired a second mortgage. That, together with my future expectations, and all will be well. You'll see."

"Second mortgage?"

"Relax. It's all under control." She waved from the doorway as she left.

Unbelievable.

A knot formed in Sam's stomach. More debt and more bills for her to pay. "Yeah, you'd better find a rich husband!" she hollered to Tiffany's long-gone figure.

Sam glanced in the mirror. She'd long since accepted what others had called her—a plain girl, colorless. Who was she kidding? Mousy brown hair, and a nose that was way too big in her opinion. She tossed the dried-up mascara tube back into the drawer and headed to the bathroom.

Minutes later, makeup scrubbed off, she went downstairs to help with dinner and found her stepmother pulling a roasted chicken from the oven.

"Something smells good." Sam snatched up an oven mitt. "Here. Let me." She took the heavy roasting pan from Katherine. "You should insist Tiff stay and help. It's shameful the way she treats you."

"I know I should," Katherine said.

"And you know I'd do more around here if I could, but my new job has taken me away more than I'd like."

"You have nothing to apologize for," Katherine said, as she placed a fork at each plate. "I so appreciate the funds you bring into this family. Your father would be so proud of you."

At sixty-three, her stepmother was still a lovely woman. Tall and slender with her pleasantly dyed hair swept up in a soft knot at the back of her head. As much as Sam tried to copy it, hers always came out severe and unflattering. She'd never known her own mother, but the photos revealed a young woman just as lovely as Katherine.

Her father certainly had great taste in women. But somewhere in Sam's line the beauty gene had skipped over her. Only a year younger than Tiffany, she'd been forever compared to her stepsister's looks. Always lacking, never quite as pretty or as slender or as feminine.

Never.

Never.

Never.

"Why do you put up with it?" Sam continued. "You should insist she stay."

"I know, I'm to fault. I'd hoped your father would have been able to rein her in. But sadly, his passing shortly after we'd married denied her the guidance she sorely needed. Four months under his care hadn't been long enough."

Katherine scooped the carrots and potatoes onto her plate. "He was such a good man. Even though our marriage had been one of convenience, it was based on mutual respect. Tiffany needed a father and you a mother. We had such high hopes for the two of you to grow up as sisters. We were both of the mind only children should not be alone."

Even though Sam had heard it all before, she nodded and sighed at all the appropriate parts in the story.

After she finished, her stepmother looked at her with a serious expression. "Tiffany hasn't been the best sister to you. I'm sorry for that. And sorry I didn't do a better job of controlling her when she was younger. I know she can be mean and spiteful. And how you've tolerated her behavior all these years is beyond me."

Sam wondered how Katherine seemed to ignore her own hand in Tiffany's treatment of her all these years. At this point in her stepmother's health, her forgetfulness was a rare occurrence. The doctor had told them it was too early to determine if her memory lapses were due to stress or something more serious.

Whether her recollections were selective or not remained to be seen. Maybe it was a good thing the woman seemed to have forgotten her role in much of

Sam's painful childhood. Sam still had a fondness for her in spite of that fact and would do her best to help her through this sad, memory-stealing condition. She hoped for her stepmother's sake, that only the good memories would linger until the end.

She placed her hand on Katherine's and gently squeezed. "Don't you worry about me. I'm a big girl now and take care of myself."

Sam hoped to reassure Katherine, but Tiffany's vindictive impulses had only gotten more unpleasant with age. She hoped her stepsister would marry and leave this house for good. And she had no intention of ever living off Tiffany's relationships.

Sam sliced a piece of chicken and forked it. "Before I forget, my new security job will have me spending the next two weeks away from home. Including most of the evenings. They've acquired a room for me at The Carlyle Hotel. If you can't reach me by phone, then leave a message for me there. Some of my work may even take place out of town. But I'll do my best to check in with you when I can." She slipped the hot morsel between her lips.

"Sounds like you'll be getting paid overtime for this one."

"I believe so."

'Good."

"Will you be okay by yourself?

"Of course. I'll speak to Tiffany. She only leaves because she knows you'll be around." Katherine patted her hand. "You're a good girl. Dependable and she knows that. But you're not to worry about me. I can still take care of myself, too."

Later that night in her attic bedroom, dressed in one of her dad's t-shirts and an old pair of soccer shorts, Sam sat on the edge of the bed, grabbed the latest tabloid, and turned to the article on Prince Marcus.

Surrounded by security and throngs of paparazzi, the photographer captured his handsome, smiling face as he made his way out of the airport into the waiting limo.

Questions surrounding who the prince's latest would be on this trip, seemed to be the bulk of the expose´, listing several female celebrities who could be in the running. Farther down, the article described his past escapades leaving each hotel suite worse off than the one before. Granted, he'd only been in his twenties, but still.

She closed the tabloid and tossed it aside, got up and rummaged through her closet until she found the stack of magazines she'd saved over the years, containing articles about the prince.

She set them at the foot of her bed, then took out the poster from the back of the closet. After pinning the top edge on the wall, she carefully unrolled it, pressing her hand along the edges before securing the bottom in place.

She ran her gaze over the scotch tape, now yellowed with age. She'd used it to repair the tear put there by Tiffany during one of her hateful outbursts.

She searched through the stack of tabloids until she found her absolute favorite article on him—in an old *Fifteen Magazine.* Twelve at the time, she reveled in all things Prince Marcus.

This particular article spoke of his work with Orphans of Ghana. A charity started by his late father, King Maxwell of Sterlyn, giving guidance and support to disadvantaged children.

Over the years, she'd so admired his commitment to carry on what his father could not. His actions were honorable and totally princely, and she'd adored him for it. She'd followed him throughout her early teens, even learning to make tea and holding secret tea parties in her room dreaming of what his life must be like.

Since that time, something had obviously changed him. She raised her gaze to the large poster hanging near the foot of her bed.

Sixteen-year-old Prince Marcus eyed her with a seductive gleam from the glossy paper. Neither the tear, nor the frayed edges took away from the heart-stopping photo. His boyish charm had melted the hearts of thousands if not millions of teenage girls, hers included.

She thought of the many lonely Friday nights she'd spent in this very room gazing at the young prince. Injecting herself into his royal world, happily escaping reality.

How many hours did she lie on this very bed, staring at this very poster, and dream of being rescued by this young prince? And in her darkest moments, even allowing her teenage heart to believe it would someday come true.

The irony of her current situation wasn't lost on her and she smiled. It was a good thing she didn't know then what she knew now—fairy tales were for children, nothing more than a coping mechanism, because reality was just too painful.

"What happened to you?" A small ache tugged at her heart. "You have everything and yet you're not satisfied."

She guessed the old saying was true...

You should never meet your heroes.

CHAPTER 5

It had been over a week since Sam had visited Oakland Manor. It was still early, and since the prince hadn't given her an actual time to start each day, she decided to make a quick stop to check on the nine residents.

She parked her old Volkswagen Beetle in front of the house and got out. The crisp December air filled her nostrils as she hurried up the wide steps to the entrance. Once inside she shrugged out of her coat expecting to be hailed from across the parlor by one or more of the residents. But all was quiet.

The Christmas tree stood in the center of the hall, its sad branches in dire need of more ornaments and lights. Making a mental note to grab some extra trimmings from home, she glanced left toward the parlor expecting to find some of the gang in there, but found it empty, as well. From the smell of bacon coming from the kitchen, she realized they were all at breakfast.

As she crossed the wide entryway, she spotted a petite lady mounting the curved staircase.

"Good morning, Miss Bette," Sam said.

Her hand on the banister, the elderly woman paused and turned.

"Oh, I'm sorry. You're not Bette."

"That's quite all right, dear." Sam was met with an engaging smile and eyes that twinkled as if delighted to see her. Warmth invaded Sam's being, and she found herself drawn to the lady's presence. Unable to help herself she stepped toward the woman.

"I don't believe we've met. I'm Sam Keller."

"Sam. Short for Samantha, I take it."

"Yes ma'am, it is. And your name?"

"My name is Elenore Terry, but my friends call me Ellie."

"Are you a new resident or just visiting?"

"Oh, I've been in and out of here for years."

"In and out? I'm sorry, what—"

"I live on the top floor and usually keep to myself. Would you like to come up for a cup of tea?"

"I'd love to, but I have to get to work. I only stopped in to say hello. Maybe another time."

"Another time, then."

The woman turned and continued to make her way up the grand staircase.

After Sam made an appearance in the kitchen, she exited the home, clipped down the steps to her car and got in.

As she drove to The Carlyle, she thought about the charming little old lady and wondered why she hadn't seen her before. Sam had been a regular volunteer at the manor and had never seen, much less *heard*, of an Ellie living there.

* * *

Marcus stood outside Samantha's room and knocked.

Samantha opened the door. "I'm almost ready." She turned back into the room and snatched up the low-heeled pumps.

"Why aren't you staying here at the hotel?"

"How did you know I haven't been staying here?"

"Eliza. She was very forthcoming and quite concerned when you didn't come back last night."

"I'm sorry, but I had to check in on my stepmother and because of the hour I decided to stay at home."

"I'd prefer it if you'd stay here. We have much to do and I'll need you to be available on short notice."

"Fine." She slipped on the pumps, then stood. "Ready for my next lesson on decorum, Your Highness."

He huffed a sigh and held the door for her to pass through.

"What *is* the next lesson?" she asked.

"The waltz."

"I don't dance... I mean I've never—"

He held out his hand and gave her a look that said she had no choice in the matter.

"Okay, fine. I'll learn the dance, if I can stay at home on the nights I need to. Deal?"

Marcus tried to outstare her, but Samantha Keller was a stubborn woman. "You have a deal," he said, walking to the center of the room. "Let's begin."

"One, two, three. One, two—Ouch, nope. That's my foot," Marcus said.

"Sorry. I have two left feet."

"One cannot waltz with two left feet."

"My point exactly."

He strode over to the portable record player provided by the hotel, then repositioned the arm over the album.

She shook her head. "This relic is a bit outdated, isn't it? Especially for such a worldly prince as yourself."

"It's a reproduction provided by the hotel manager. And it is you who is outdated. These beauties are back in style."

As the beginning notes of The Blue Danube permeated the royal suite, he strode back to the center of the room.

"The waltz is one of the most beautiful and romantic dances in the world. If you would simply try to relax. Your problem is you will not let me lead."

"Let you lead? I don't even know which way to go, so how can I lead?"

"Let me say it another way. You're fighting me. You're stiff, tense. Afraid to let down your guard."

She sucked in a deep breath, then blew it out. "Fine." She lifted both of her arms in the ready.

He closed the gap between them, his face mere inches from hers.

"Left hand on my shoulder," he said, placing his right hand firmly against her lower back. Then clasping her right hand in his left, he gazed into her upturned face.

"Ready?"

She licked her lips and nodded.

"Close your eyes."

"But?"

"Close. Your. Eyes."

She let out a shaky breath and did as he asked.

"Have I told you how much I hate this?"

"At least a dozen times already," he said. "Now. Listen to the rhythm. One... Two... Three. Trust your feelings. Don't over think it."

"Okay."

She stood, with her eyes squeezed shut, tense and waiting with a pained look on her face that suddenly struck him as adorable. He'd never in his life met a woman as self-deprecating, honest to a fault, and completely irresistible as Samantha Keller.

"You might find it helpful to breathe," he said.

Eyes still closed, she shuddered an exhale and nervously licked her lips.

With his gaze on her face, he stepped forward and her left foot moved back.

"That's it. Step along with me. Go where I lead."

With his hand securely at her back, he deftly maneuvered her smoothly across the floor, keeping to the three-quarter time. When the music came to an end, Sam's eyes fluttered open revealing a childlike magic in their depths.

"You see? Easy."

"For you, maybe."

"One more time?"

"Sure."

This time she came into his arms as if she'd done it many times before. And except for a couple of missteps, she followed his lead, albeit, a bit clumsily. Even so, the intimacy in the dance was not lost as he applied the subtle, but necessary pressure against her lower back. He felt her relax, felt her stiffness melt away, felt her confidence soar with every step she took while in his arms.

When the music stopped, she gazed at him, breathless, bright-eyed and triumphant—completely unaware of the captivating picture she made. In that moment, Samantha Keller was completely irresistible and her joy, contagious.

"You're a natural. With a bit more practice everyone will believe you've been dancing like this most of your life."

Her cheeks, still flush from the dance, deepened to a rosy hue at his praise. For a moment they stood arm in arm as if waiting to start the dance again. Reluctantly, he released her. She lowered her gaze and stepped back. Something tangible had passed between them. He'd felt it and wondered if she had as well.

CHAPTER 6

Sunday afternoon, Sam lifted the large box of Christmas decorations from the back seat of her VW Bug, then kicked the door shut with her left foot. Peeking around the side of the box, she mounted the steps to the manor. As she reached for the handle, Bette had already beaten her to it, opening the door wide.

Seeing Bette made Sam think of Miss Ellie. She wondered if the little lady would gather for the rest of the tree trimming or stay in her room.

Once inside, Sam set the box near the tree and removed her wool overcoat. Florence and Theo, the only married couple in the residence, had opened the box and were now in the process of untangling the twinkle lights. Bette had gone to round up the others interested in helping.

A few minutes later, the aroma of buttered popcorn drifted down the hall from the kitchen and Miss Clara stood nearby filling teacups with hot chocolate.

Over the next couple of hours Miss Ellie never showed. Once the tree trimming was close to being finished, Sam suggested they take a break and watch a movie. After the residents started watching *It's A Wonderful Life*, Sam made her way to the upstairs room.

She reached the apartment and tapped lightly on the oak door.

"Samantha." Miss Ellie beamed and took hold of her hands. "I've been wondering when you were going to come."

Sam stepped through the threshold into the most magical little room she'd ever seen. A fire burned in the grate and twinkle lights hung from every corner of the apartment. It was like stepping into a giant snow globe.

"Who did all of this for you?"

"Maintenance," Miss Ellie said.

Above the grate was a small mantel which housed a collection of black and white photographs Sam assumed were Miss Ellie's friends and family members.

"Is that a Tony award?"

"Yes, for my work on the Broadway version of *Cinderella*."

"That is way cool."

"Thank you, dear."

"We all missed you downstairs. You should come see the tree."

"I promise, but first...tea."

Minutes later, Miss Ellie returned from the kitchen with a pot of hot water and her tea tray.

"I see you've been admiring my photographs," she said.

"They're fascinating pictures. I especially love the gowns you and the other ladies are wearing in this one."

"Those are my designs."

"You're kidding."

Miss Ellie shook her head. "Many years ago, I started out in fashion. That Emmy was for my dress designs for the ballroom scene in *Cinderella*. Later, I discovered the stage and I added acting to my world. But what about you? Why do you dress like a man?"

"Um."

"And why do you wear your hair like that? All skinned back in some old woman's bun. You're in the prime of your life."

Sam lifted her hand to the back of her head. "You don't mince words, do you, Miss Ellie."

"You have such lovely high cheekbones. With a face like yours, *you* could be on the stage."

What an odd thing for her to say.

"What is it about beauty that frightens you so?"

"I'm not frightened."

"You've obviously put up a wall, as if you wish to hide your beauty."

The conversation seemed so out of left field. The scary thing? Miss Ellie was more right than wrong. The years of standing in Tiffany's shadow, not measuring up, made it easier to create a wall of protection around herself. A way of self-preservation.

Speechless, she gazed at the older woman, then blinked and swallowed. "Man, I sure could've used you in my life years ago. Thank you for saying so, but I'm no beauty." Hoping like crazy to change the subject she focused her attention to the dessert tray. "Those little cakes look yummy."

Miss Ellie smiled. "I see you're also adept at deflection."

Sam's mouth opened in denial, and when she could think of no come-back, she sat down.

Miss Ellie leaned across the small round table, placed her finger at Sam's temple and tapped twice. "You are the author of your life. Even though others have tried to compose it. Remember, it's you who writes your own story. How you think of yourself is who you are. How you react to what life throws at you is your choice, no one else's."

Sam shook her head, amazed at this wise and fiery little woman.

"Are you sure you're not a psychologist?"

"No dear."

"Even though what you say is true, you don't know me. I admit that I've allowed the opinion of others to... sway me. Although at the time, I didn't realize it."

"You were a child."

"Yes, but how did you—"

"So much of what we come to believe about ourselves is a result of our childhood experiences. But how you react is the key. Take this tea bag. What happens to the tea when you steep the bag for a long time?"

"Really, I've heard this before—"

"Answer the question."

"It becomes stronger." She answered dutifully feeling like a school girl.

"How hot does the water have to be?"

Sam grinned. "Very."

"The hotter the water, the stronger the tea. The young woman I see before me has been steeped in hot water, more than once. Right?"

"I guess so." Sam shrugged.

"And I can see you're a strong woman. But even the strong can believe a lie."

Completely and utterly uncomfortable, Sam lifted the cup to her lips, wondering how this woman could know so much about her. She took a sip, then grimaced.

Miss Ellie plucked up a sugar cube and with the utmost timing of a seasoned stage actress, gently plopped it in Sam's cup—as if her action had been chore-

ographed for that very moment. "And most importantly, the strong can become bitter without the addi-
tion of something sweet."

Sam lifted the sweetened tea to her mouth and
sipped.

"Better?"

"Better." She set the cup down and focused on the
petite lady sitting opposite. "You're a woman of wisdom and yet you closet yourself away from the rest of
the world. Why?"

Ellie patted Sam's hand, then stood. "I must leave
that story for another day."

Sam left in a bit of a daze. What a remarkable lady.
What she wouldn't have given to have had such a person in her life during her growing up years. She liked
to think her mother would have been such a woman.

* * *

Monday morning, Percy handed Marcus a copy of
his itinerary for the upcoming week, while Samantha
sat opposite cradling a cup of coffee in her hands.

"This evening's gala opens your two-week visit,"
Percy said. "Tomorrow evening's red-carpet dinner-
dance is in Scarsdale. Wednesday at noon, the mayor
is presenting you the key to the city. The Royal Holiday
Tea follows in the hotel's green room at two o'clock."

"And where's the mayor's presentation taking place?"

"On the steps of New York City Hall."

"Got it."

"The unveiling of King Maxwell's statue at Meadowbrook Polo Club takes place at five o'clock on Thursday, followed by a wine tasting, then dinner. And Friday has been left open for Christmas shopping, as you requested."

"And the preparations for next week's Christmas Eve gala?"

"The hotel management has assured me all is on schedule."

"Good."

"I'm sorry, but aren't you supposed to be going back home before Christmas?" Sam asked.

"I've decided to extend my stay until after."

"Has my position been extended, as well?"

"Yes."

"Without clearing it with me?"

He cocked his head to the side. "I'm sorry, is that going to be a problem?"

"It so happens that it's not. But it's your assumption that everyone is at your beck and call that—"

"Not everyone, just you." He grinned, knowing it would madden her.

She gave a quick nod and went into her efficient, security officer mode. "May I see the list?"

"Of course." Marcus handed her his copy.

He watched her peruse the sheet. Her hair had been gently pulled away from her face, falling in soft waves around her shoulders. Eliza had arranged for a salon visit resulting in the golden highlights in Sam's light brown hair. The result of which flattered her features beautifully.

"I see the days leading up to the Christmas Eve Gala are filled with similar activities as this coming week," she said. "What about adding a visit to a charity? If you really want to change how people view you, then you should add something more, oh...you know, down to earth. Something to take the focus off you."

He quirked a smile. "Miss Keller, is this payback for my earlier assumption, or are you simply trying to change my image?"

"You did say you wanted to do something worthwhile for someone less fortunate while you were in town." She glanced at the itinerary. "All I see here are purely social and..."

"Self-gratifying pursuits?" he said.

A pink hue covered her cheeks as she stuttered an incoherent reply. "Well...I...I wouldn't have put it that way."

"It's all right. Believe it or not, I agree with you. Any suggestions?"

"Actually, yes." She licked her lips. "There's a retirement home in Richmond Hill. In Queens. There're only a handful of residents, most of whom have little or no visitors to speak of. Christmas is especially difficult for them. I'd suggest a visit. Simple at first. No fanfare or cameras. Just you and me. If and when it's discovered, the press will see a side of you they didn't know was there. Or at least had forgotten about. And who knows, maybe you'll be moved to do something for the residents while you're in town."

"Without the media, how will me going help change my image?"

"I didn't say there'd be no media. Just leave it to me."

CHAPTER 7

The ballroom at The Carlyle Hotel sparkled like jewels glistening in the moonlight. Christmas trees hugged the corners in groups of threes while twinkling white lights hung from the ceiling like rain. Clusters of silver and gold ornaments scattered throughout the room added a regal element to the festive atmosphere. Sam had never seen anything like it and stood taking in the fairy tale wonder of it all.

She had long since made certain the room was secure even though Marcus had insisted she not worry about it. He'd assured her his people were fully capable of protecting him.

Uncomfortably dressed in a below the knee red chiffon dress, she entered the ornate room only minutes before the prince was to be announced. She'd balked when Eliza held the dress out to her, insisting she at least try it on. She did, and the sleeveless, low cut clingy material made her feel half naked.

Eliza had clucked over her, exclaiming how lovely she looked and that His Highness would be so pleased.

Sam's first instinct had been to take it off right then and there, but something about the skimpiness of the dress and the curve-revealing fabric made her *feel* beautiful. Something she'd rarely, if ever, felt. A heady sensation for one used to being the ugly duckling in the family.

She'd raised her chin, telling herself she could do this. Hadn't she dreamed of this very thing as a twelve-year-old, gazing with acute longing at his poster?

But now, in the ballroom with so many in atten-dance, she wasn't so sure. And as a self-proclaimed duck, she was way out of water and feeling anything, but confident.

Better to focus on the job at hand. As she waited for the prince's arrival, she gave herself a mental shake and scanned the guests in attendance. Aside from the mayor and a few celebrities, she had no clue who the rest of them were.

Known for his hobnobbing with the rich and fa-mous, she wondered who the prince would have on his arm when he entered the ballroom. Some Hollywood or Broadway star, most likely. He was in New York City, after all.

At that moment a man dressed in a black tuxedo appeared at the entrance. "May I present His Royal Highness, Prince Marcus de Blecourt of Sterlyn."

The prince appeared in the gilded doorway, *alone*, with no stunning beauty at his side. Dressed in the colorful uniform of Captain, Sterlyn Guards, he was magnificent. All meticulous and regal, he took her breath away.

He was every bit the prince. From the red coat regaled in gold caplets and cuffs to the cobalt blue sash that angled, from shoulder to hip, across his chest.

Marcus strolled in and around his guests, shaking hands, and pausing briefly to speak to several on his way to the dance floor.

As if on cue, the string quartet began to play a slow waltz. Sam stepped back along with those around her to see who he'd approach. One of the Hollywood celebs no doubt. She glanced right and then left, then back toward him.

Oh. My. Gosh. He was heading straight for her. No, no, no! She wasn't ready. It was too soon!

Mouth suddenly dry, she found herself staring up at Marcus as he held out his hand to her. She made a desperate attempt to communicate a big fat no with her eyes and got nowhere. The seconds that passed felt like an eternity as a hushed silence fell across the ballroom. And just when she thought she'd embarrassed them both, she placed her hand in his. May as well take the humiliation to the next level.

So, this was it. She'd known from the beginning she wouldn't be up to the job. No time like the present to prove that to the prince and the rest of the world.

Dazed, she allowed him to lead her onto the dance floor.

"You've got this." Marcus spoke softly as he placed his hand to her back. Taking her other, he expertly led and twirled her around.

Acutely aware that every eye watched her, she did her best to block that image and to concentrate on her feet.

One, two, three, repeated over and over in her mind like an amusement park ride. Marcus twirled and turned her across the dance floor until the people on the sidelines faded into one, long, circular blur. Until she blocked out everything but...

The smile in his eyes.

The warmth of his hand at her waist.

The width of his shoulders, his slightly parted lips and the way he gazed at her as if he knew something she did not.

So, this is what it must feel like to be beautiful and admired and a princess. To be loved and treasured by such a man as Marcus de Blecourt of Sterlyn would be heavenly indeed, but until now had only existed in her dreams. The dreams of an awkward, teenage girl.

He was far above her reach. Completely out of her league. But could it be possible, just this once, for her dreams to come true?

The music stopped, breaking the spell, and the prince led her off to the sidelines as several guests took to the dance floor.

"You were fantastic," he said. "You held every eye in the room."

"That's what worries me. I don't like being in the limelight."

"Too late for that, Miss Keller."

He laid an irresistibly devastating grin on her and she wanted to sock him one.

"That's right. Go ahead and laugh. Everything's a joke with you."

His smile quickly faded, and his eyes flashed with annoyance. She blinked and dropped her gaze, realizing she'd probably gone too far. She was, after all, in his employ, and if he fired her, she'd lose her job at the agency.

But his anger quickly turned to compassion as if he understood the position he'd placed her in.

"I do apologize if I've caused you discomfort, but as I recall you took this job with the understanding that you'd be in the public eye. Is that not true?"

She nodded. "I'm also sorry if my words insulted you."

"It's quite all right." He glanced over his shoulder. "I must see to my guests. And may I suggest you stop frowning and try to enjoy the rest of the evening. The media is prone to exaggeration and no telling what that furrow between your lovely eyes will lead them to believe."

He lifted her right hand, gently pressed his lips against it, then walked away.

* * *

Marcus left Samantha standing on the sidelines. It was obvious to him she needed time to recover. Frankly, he'd not been prepared for that pleading stare of hers, telling...no demanding he not dance with her. As much as he'd wished that he hadn't approached her for the first dance, he couldn't very well back out. The papers would have written it as a snub, making him a laughingstock.

No one ever said no to a prince simply asking for a dance. Samantha's hesitation was bad enough, and thankfully, it seemed to go without notice by the press.

Due to the lack of time and his mission to rid himself of Pricilla, he'd realized too late the pressure he'd placed on her and despised himself for his insensitivity.

Getting Samantha up to the standards expected by those in his circles had not been the challenge he'd first surmised. These past few days in her company, working closely with her, he began to see the real person behind the mask and the false front she'd presented to the world around her.

Frankly, it was the reason he'd danced with her instead of someone else. But it wasn't until her near refusal that he realized the issue wasn't her lack of ability but her lack of self-confidence.

Yes, he'd thrown her in the deep end, fully aware of her discomfort. But having seen a glimpse of the real Samantha Keller, he knew she'd be able to survive. She was a fighter. If anyone could give Priscilla a what for, it was this feisty New Yorker.

While in her company, he'd found himself growing more attracted to her each day. Even with her daily, battle-ready facade, he could tell there was more to her than she presented to the world around her. Something hidden.

Someone, he wished to discover.

A challenge he would like to explore. Another time, maybe. But right now, it was far safer to keep going with the ruse. It wouldn't do to get emotionally involved with one woman while trying to rid himself of another.

* * *

Sam had decided to spend the night at the hotel. After all, it had been secured for her use, and since the gala went well into the evening hours, she took advantage of it.

It was 2:00 a.m. when she crawled into the four-poster bed. Even though it was late, she found it difficult to fall asleep.

The prince had danced with her two more times, as well as the female celebrities and dignitaries present. Even the mayor's wife had enjoyed a spin with him around the ballroom. Courteous and thoughtful, he was the perfect host.

And the food was fabulous. She enjoyed dishes she'd only heard of or read about in magazines.

The evening had been like something out of a story book, and she would cherish it for the rest of her life. She turned to her side, closed her eyes and pushed back against her childhood fantasies surrounding the prince.

Tonight had been filled with magic and glitter and had made her believe happily ever after could very well someday be hers, but certainly not with a prince.

CHAPTER 8

Marcus sat down to breakfast as Percy delivered the morning paper.

"Thank you, Percy. I take it from that scowl we made the society page."

"That and then some, Your Highness."

"So, my evil plan is working." Marcus turned to the section in question to find a full-page photo of him dancing with Samantha." They were gazing into each other's eyes like lovers. "Excellent," he said. "I should commend the photographer. He caught the perfect moment."

"May I point out, neither Parliament, nor your mother will be pleased."

"Nor will Pricilla."

"Begging your pardon, sir, but knowing Pricilla, it will take more than a photograph to keep her from the altar."

"Don't forget, I have to be standing there in order for a wedding to take place."

"Sterlyn law states you cannot be crowned king unless you are married."

"Of which I'm well aware." Marcus continued to stare at the photograph as he ran a finger across his bottom lip.

At that precise moment Samantha stormed through the adjoining door.

"Have you seen this morning's paper?"

He squinted against the high-pitched shrill in her voice. Eyes enormously wide and filled with something between anxiety and smoldering anger, she marched across the room ready for battle. He wondered if in her haste, she'd forgotten that she still wore pajamas. Very pretty pink, long sleeved ones, with pearl buttons and the royal crest embroidered over her left top pocket. She was all lovely and feminine even down to her bare feet and pink painted toenails.

"Yes, I'm aware. I just discovered it myself. Coffee?"

She plopped down across from him. Percy poured her a cup, then left.

"I believe the muffins are still warm, if you'd like to try—"

"How could this have happened?" She slapped the newspaper against the corner of the dining table. "You danced with three movie stars, for crying out loud. Why isn't one of them in the photo?"

"You'll have to ask the photographer."

She sat back, deflated. She looked so forlorn he was tempted to take her in his arms and instinctively knew he would quite enjoy doing that.

She grabbed her bottom lip with her teeth and stared at the tabletop.

Seconds later she raised her stricken gaze to his. "And who is Lady Pricilla Rothschild?"

He let out a heartfelt sigh. "I'm afraid you're not going to like the answer."

"Tell me."

"Lady Pricilla expects to be the next Princess of Sterlyn."

"You're engaged?" Her flushed cheeks paled.

"Not technically. I haven't asked her to marry me, although some in my country expect me to."

"Like who?"

"My mother, Mr. and Mrs. Rothschild, Parliament and basically most of Sterlyn." He glanced back over his shoulder. "Have I left anyone out, Percy?"

"I don't believe so, sir."

"This isn't funny."

"I wholeheartedly agree," he said, as he buttered a piece of toast.

Sam's eyes widened to the size of the muffin plate. "You have to fix this!" she burst out.

"What would you suggest I do?"

"I don't know. You're the prince."

"Who has no authority with the American press."

"They all want to know if I'm your...your...latest conquest?"

She snatched up a muffin and bit down.

"I'm very sorry," he said. "Listen. Let's take the day off. I have nothing scheduled that can't be rescheduled."

She kept eating and refused to look him.

"Samantha, truly, this is nothing to worry about. The press writes insane things about me all the time. Do you hate the limelight that much?"

"Yes. I don't..." She glanced away. "I can't talk about it."

"What happened?"

She shot to her feet. "I don't care what you do today, and I don't think we should be seen together."

She hurried back to her room.

Marcus stared at the closed door. "Percy. Follow her—discreetly. I want to know where she goes." He stood. "And contact Blake St. John at Colfax Security and see what you can find out about Samantha's background. It seems our no-nonsense, matter of fact, cool-headed security officer has just fallen apart."

* * *

Sam stepped outside the hotel to find Tiffany barreling down on her.

"What the heck is this?" She smacked the society page against Sam's chest.

Sam squeezed her eyes shut, then opened them to her angry, red-faced stepsister. "A mistake. It's nothing."

"Nothing? You've been seeing the most eligible bachelor on the planet and you call that nothing?"

"I've been assigned to protect him. I'm one of his security people."

Sam marched toward the curb and raised her arm in an attempt to hail a taxi.

"Oh, this so looks like you're protecting him." Tiffany shook the photo in Sam's face. "That is the look of attraction."

"Why should you care? You've snared your wealthy yacht owner." She turned and strode down the sidewalk doing her best to put distance between them.

"Jason Osborne is no prince."

Sam spun on her heels, nearly colliding with Tiffany. "Look. I can't help when the photographer snapped that picture. Whatever you see there is not real. Why aren't you with your mother?"

"I just came from there. The paparazzi are all over our front lawn."

Great.

Sam raised her arm, snagged the next taxi and got in.

"We're not done here!" Tiffany yelled.

On the way home all Sam could think about was that ill-timed photo and all of those questions about her identity. Questions which would lead to answers. And answers that would come back to haunt her and disgrace Colfax Security.

She leaned her head against the back seat and closed her eyes. The media will never let this go. It'll be all over the city and maybe even the country by mid-day. Blake St. John would have to fire her, if for nothing else, but to save his business.

When she got to her house, it was as Tiff had said. The media had set up shop in their front yard. At her request, the driver pulled in and drove to the back of the property. She paid him and got out. As she made a dash to the back door, reporters swarmed and peppered her with questions.

"How did you meet the prince?"

"What's your relationship to him?"

"How do you think Lady Rothschild will react to the news?"

Sam ducked and ran up the steps, then hurled herself through the back door as the reporters barked more questions.

"Katherine!" she yelled.

"In here."

Sam found her stepmother in the front parlor peeking out through the blinds.

"Are you all right?"

"Yes, but what's this about? Why's the media here?"

"Didn't Tiffany tell you?"

"No, she just up and left."

"I'm in the newspaper. The man I'm protecting is a...celebrity." Leery to tell Katherine all the facts, she left it at that. Tiffany would most likely fill her in later.

"There was a party in his honor, and we danced... and the photographer took our picture. It's now in the paper."

"I see."

"You know how these celebrity things are. I'm sure it'll die down in a day or so. If not, I'll quit my job and hopefully this will all go away."

"Quit? That doesn't sound like you."

"Maybe so, but—"

"We need your income, Sam. It's not like you to be selfish."

"Believe me, what they'll write could hurt us more than a job loss."

"It will only hurt you. After all, we're not blood related."

She stiffened. There it was. The selfish stepmother she used to know. She choked back the pain of Katherine's hateful words.

"Have you eaten?" Was all Sam could think to ask.

"I think you should leave. Afterward, I'll speak to them. Tell them you've gone."

"No. Do not open that door. I'll go if you want, but don't open the door or speak to them. Promise me."

Katherine gave a curt nod and turned away.

Sam ran up the stairs to her room. She placed her hand over her mouth and pressed her back against the wall. Is this what her life had come to. Homeless? Jobless? The possibility of both loomed in front of her.

She'd go to Oakland Manor. At least the people there genuinely cared for her. She'd spend the day with them, then decide what to do.

CHAPTER 9

Marcus took a taxi to the address Percy had sent him. An area called, Queens. He paid the driver, then stood for a moment on the opposite side of the street, gazing at a charming Victorian house. It was in need of repair, but even from this distance, he could tell the structure was solid and well-built.

He waited near a large Maple tree until the last of the media had gone. He glanced right, then left. Assured all was clear, he crossed the street, then headed up the sidewalk.

Boxwoods bordered the narrow pathway which opened to a wide set of steps and a deep front porch encased in what certainly looked to be handcrafted millwork.

Marcus had shared his father's passion for the delicate, spiral-turreted houses and would have enjoyed restoring such a home with him.

Once at the front door, he knocked. As he waited, he continued to admire the delicate, hand-carved millwork. An attractive older woman finally answered. She seemed hesitant and peered around him as if looking for someone else.

"May I help you?" she asked.

"Yes. I'm looking for Samantha Keller. Is she here?"

"No. She's gone and has no wish to speak to the media."

As she made an attempt to shut the door, he lifted his hand. "I'm not the media. I'm a friend. I wanted to see if she was all right."

"I wouldn't know. She's brought trouble to this house, so I sent her away."

"And you are...?"

"Her stepmother."

"I see. Well, I'm sorry to have bothered you."

Without another word, the woman closed the door in his face.

As he made his way down the steps, he checked his phone to find Percy had left a message with an address. He punched the house number and street name into Maps on his phone and waited for the app to load. The display read, Oakland Manor. The house was only a few blocks away. Close enough to walk.

As he took off in the direction displayed in the app, he marveled at the charming neighborhood. Victorian houses were prominent to the area and he could tell most of them had been well maintained.

At one time houses like this had been plentiful in Sterlyn, until those with more modern ideas started tearing them down. Thankfully his father had put a stop to it, declaring the style as one of the country's architectural treasures. Having done so, he set in motion their restoration, having added them to Sterlyn's historic registry, which Marcus himself now chaired.

Five minutes later, he mounted the steps of Oakland Manor. He stepped into the warmth of the old home and shook off the chill from the cold December wind. The aroma of cinnamon and pine wafted through the air, welcoming him.

As he slipped off his coat and gloves, he glanced around the large, high-ceilinged room. After tossing them on a chair in the foyer, he continued inside.

A Christmas tree glowed with multi-colored lights and old-fashion glass ornaments, while a fire burned and crackled in what looked to be a sitting room. Several elderly people sat throughout the area sipping from teacups and playing board games.

A middle aged, pleasant-looking woman approached him.

"Hi there. Welcome. I'm Caroline Hill. I manage the home. Are you here to visit one of our residents?"

"No, I'm a friend of Samantha Keller. I understand she volunteers on Sundays. I was told she'd be here today."

"Yes, she's around somewhere. Come on in."

He followed Caroline as far as the Christmas tree and waited. This must be the retirement home Samantha had suggested he visit.

Everything, from the walls to the furniture, looked old and worn, but the residents didn't seem to mind as they visited amongst themselves like family.

"Marcus."

He turned at the sound of Samantha's voice.

"What are you doing here? I told you—"

"Making sure you're okay."

"How did you find me?"

"After you left, I had Percy follow you."

She glared at him. "You had no right."

"Please don't be angry. I'd still like to spend the rest of the day together." He made a point of looking around. "I don't see any cameras or media of any kind. No one is here to document my visit. It'll be just as you suggested. Unless you've changed your mind about my coming and helping in some way."

She glanced at her shoes then over at the handful of residents already decorating the mantel. "Okay, but if you stay, you'll work. I could use your help stringing garland on the staircase."

"I'd like that."

He followed her to the large box and looked inside. "It's real."

"Of course, it's real. Oakland Manor wouldn't have it any other way. Don't you use real greenery at your castle?"

"Absolutely. I meant no ill will with my earlier comment. I just assumed, due to the state of the property, that artificial decorations would be more economical."

He pulled out a long strand. "Where would you like to start? Up top?"

"Right here is fine. We can work our way up."

They worked together tucking and looping and tying off sections as they mounted the staircase. He periodically glanced at her profile. Glum-faced and pensive she worked quietly—unsmiling and obviously worried about something.

"I stopped by your house on the way here."

Samantha stilled and lifted her gaze to his. "You went to my house?"

"Yes, and I had the uh...pleasure of meeting your stepmother."

She continued to stare at him as if expecting him to say more, then dropped her gaze.

"I see." She attached a large red bow to the railing. "There was a time I wouldn't have wished her on my worst enemy."

"But not now?"

"She's suffering from memory loss. Sometimes she can say the kindness things to me, then other times..." She shrugged.

"She told me she sent you away. What did she mean by that?"

"She meant for me not to come back."

"That's terrible."

"It is, but tomorrow she may not even remember having said it to me."

He helped her attach another bow, then mounted the next few steps behind her.

"From now on, I want you to stay in the hotel while I'm in town. After all, it was the original arrangement I set up with Colfax Security."

"Thank you, but I don't think it's a good idea for me to work for you anymore."

At the top of the stairs they tied off the last of the garland and red bows in silence.

"I'm sorry to hear that. Look. Is there someplace we can talk?"

"There's a sitting area on the next level. We could talk there, if you'd like."

The upper landing was comprised of two small fabric covered chairs and a love seat tucked beneath a large bay window. A wooden floor lamp with an off-white shade edged in fringe stood between one of the chairs and the small sofa.

They sat down next to each other on the love seat. Samantha turned her gaze toward him and waited.

"Before you decide to quit, I'd like to explain about Pricilla. It's true that she's my betrothed, but in name only. I don't love her, never have. She and I have known each other most of our lives. I'm fond of her, but that's as far as it goes."

He stretched his arm along the back of the sofa, angling toward her. "We've shared many experiences over the years, but that's no reason to marry."

"Surely you have the right to choose your own bride."

The sincerity in her gaze touched him.

"One would think. Years ago, my parents and hers thought it would be a good idea to join our two families through marriage, and it was understood that Pricilla and I would someday wed."

"So, it's an arranged marriage."

"Not in the way you're thinking, but over the years it became an expected thing. Our families assumed we'd grow up and agree. Pricilla has agreed, but I have not.

"I'm pressured from some quarters to do so and if I refuse it will humiliate the Rothschilds. The last thing I want is to dishonor the family with whom we've shared such long-standing friendship."

"You're an honorable man." She twisted her hands together in her lap. "I can see why you'd struggle with your decision."

"Over the past several years, I've adopted a lifestyle in public as a playboy prince in hopes Pricilla will back out of the assumed arrangement, thus saving face for her and that of her family."

"I see."

"I told you at our first meeting that I needed you to protect me from someone. That someone is Pricilla. So far, my bachelor antics haven't deterred her one little bit. It's as if she knows the game I'm playing. Pricilla has hounded, and cajoled, and manipulated long enough. She won't take no for an answer."

"She sounds like an incurable disease."

He chuckled, nodding. "That's where you come in. You are the antidote against Pricilla Rothschild."

"I don't know." Her brow furrowed and she glanced down.

"You wouldn't have to do anything, just go on as before. The media already thinks you're my special someone, so why tell them any differently."

"I'd like to help you, really but—"

"If Pricilla believes you and I are the real thing, then she'll have no course but to abandon any thoughts of marrying me."

"I doubt that if what you say about her is true."

"She's a prideful woman. It's one thing to ignore my harmless flings, but if she believes I'm in a serious relationship and the media confirms that, then trust me, she will not do anything to make herself look bad."

She lightly fingered a loose tendril of hair on her cheek. "Sooo, we just go on as before and let the press say what they want about us?"

"Yes. You, who could care less for my title or position. From the moment you stormed out of my suite, your forthright 'in your face' attitude told me you were the one for the job."

"And that's the reason for all the clothes and hair styles, the makeup and dance lessons?"

"And the table manners, don't forget."

She rolled her eyes. "How could I?"

He grabbed hold of her hands and gave them a quick shake. "I'm teasing you."

Her lips twitched into a beguiling smile, and she shook her head.

"But I can see you're still worried about something," he said. "Is it your discomfort in the limelight?"

"I'm normally not so timid. It's just... Something happened...when I was—Miss Ellie."

Ellie stood at the bottom of the third-floor staircase and seemed to appear out of nowhere.

"Goodness. I hope I didn't startle you," she said. "I've been cooped up in my room at the top of the house most of the day. Needed to stretch my legs."

She beamed at Marcus as she crossed the landing to where they were seated. "And who is this handsome young man?"

"This is Marcus. A friend of mine."

Marcus stood and took hold of Ellie's hand. "It's a pleasure to meet you."

"He's just been helping with the staircase," Sam said. "What do you think?"

Ellie peered over the railing and looked down. "It's beautiful and quite festive."

"We all missed you earlier. Bette served her famous hot chocolate."

"Speaking of sweets, would you two lovelies like to join me for caramel cake?"

Marcus and Sam glanced at each other and nodded.

They followed Ellie up the third flight of stairs, then down a short hallway to her living quarters.

He stopped abruptly at the sparkling array of twinkle lights.

Samantha chuckled. "Quite a sight isn't it?"

"I'll say." Except for the festive decor, the low ceiling suite of rooms reminded him of the attic room at the caretaker's cottage at Sterlyn Castle. He'd spent many happy hours there during his childhood while Edward and his father discussed architecture.

Until this moment, his boyhood memories had been conveniently pushed aside in pursuit of a happiness he'd come to believe was unattainable. He missed his father. Missed his wisdom, his guidance, and most of all his companionship.

"Samantha, would you be a dear and cut the caramel cake?" Ellie said, interrupting his thoughts. "It's on the kitchen table."

"Of course." Sam crossed the small room and entered the kitchen while Marcus and Miss Ellie took a seat in front of the fireplace.

"I would've liked to have had a daughter like our Samantha here," Ellie said. "One of God's good creatures, don't you agree?"

"Ah, yes. Yes, she is."

What a peculiar little lady. He liked her immediately.

A moment later, Sam entered the sitting room carrying three pieces of sliced cake on a wooden tray. After serving them, she took a seat next to Marcus.

Sam dove into the three-tiered cake with a fork, exclaiming pleasure over the dessert and smiling at something the older woman had said. For a second, Marcus watched her interact with the elderly woman. As Miss Ellie chatted, Sam's eyes never left her face. Her attention and kindness to the old woman touched him deeply. Samantha was indeed a warm and thoughtful person, displaying every attribute of a true princess. He thought about the cruel words from her stepmother. The woman didn't deserve her.

CHAPTER 10

After they said goodbye to Miss Ellie, Sam and Marcus spent another hour visiting the rest of the residents, where Sam got to witness first-hand Marcus' talent for making others feel comfortable. He sat down to a game of Hearts with her, Bette, and Sylvia, then played a quick game of checkers with Harvey.

While Harvey mulled over his next move, she pulled out her cell phone and began taking a video.

"Is this your idea of getting the word out?" Marcus said.

"You have heard of social media, right?"

"As much as you may think it, I don't live under a rock... Or in a cave."

"We'll add a special hashtag, in your honor, and post away. You'll see. It'll go viral in minutes."

"Harvey, will you be okay with all this attention?"

"Of course. I used to be on the stage, you know. Off, off Broadway." He chuckled. "Live audience or video, makes no difference to me."

"And don't worry, Marcus," she said. "I'm not saying where you are."

After their game, Marcus joined her by the tree. "This house is amazing. The oak staircase is equal to any found in Sterlyn."

"It is beautiful, but unfortunately, the manor's been sold to some developer. Caroline has been frantically searching for another place. They'd like to stay in this area, if possible." She stepped left and held up her phone. "Stand there and pretend you're adding an ornament."

"How long do the residents have before they are forced to leave?" he asked, placing his fingers around a silver ball.

"I'm not sure of the exact date but it's sometime in February."

"I'm sorry to hear that. Hopefully, something will work out."

"Hopefully." She took another photo. "Got it. You can lower your hand now."

Sam placed her phone in her purse just as the sweet strains of "Have Yourself a Merry Little Christmas" floated from the parlor.

Florence and Theo were already swaying to the poignant Christmas classic. She eyed them with a heartfelt longing, wishing she'd had the chance to watch her parents grow old together. She glanced over at Marcus who stood watching the couple.

"How charming," Marcus said.

Harvey had long since left his chair and was now leading Bette to the dance floor.

"Come over here you two," Bette said. "There's plenty of room out here."

Marcus glanced at her. "I'm game, if you are."

"Okay."

He took hold of her hand and led her to the parlor.

When they stopped, Sam faced him, and he took her in his arms.

"You know, I don't believe I've ever slow danced to a Christmas song. It's most romantic." His eyes held a twinkle as he gazed down at her.

"The song is lovely," she said. "It's a strange mixture of sad and happy."

"Melancholy, but hopeful."

He placed his hand on the back of her neck and drew her closer, giving her no choice but to rest her head on his shoulder. Not that she minded in the least.

He'd surprised her with his sensitive observation—this man with whom formality and protocol were so second-nature. She knew the prince. Sure, her knowledge of him had been limited to the tabloids and gossip rags, but she'd gladly take this as a sign that the young man she'd adored through childhood was still in there somewhere.

* * *

That evening, Sam sat next to Marcus in a black limo twirling the stem of a water glass while watching thousands of Christmas lights clip by the window. New Yorkers loved the holidays and spared no expense with their festive decorations.

"Are you sure that's all you want to drink?" he asked. "Anything to settle your nerves?"

"Water's fine."

He poured himself a glass of sherry, then settled back in the seat next to her.

"You were great this afternoon," she said. "You've won the hearts of Oakland Manor."

"And without them knowing who I really am. That's saying something."

"It must be difficult thinking people only care because of who you are. I can't imagine what it's like to have to be on all the time. Must be exhausting."

"It is. Although I do have some great friends from my time at school. People I can be myself with. And of course, there's the staff at Sterlyn Castle, most of whom I've known all my life. I consider them family, as much as I do my mother."

The prince had opened up to her, and she found herself staring at him as a result.

"What are you thinking?"

"That I'm sitting in a posh limousine with a prince." *And that you're a much nicer person than the world thinks.*

"Is that a good or bad thing?"

"Ask me at the end of next week." She glanced out of the window.

"So. You ready to tell me what happened?"

She eyed him with confusion.

"The thing you were going to tell me when Miss Ellie interrupted us."

"Oh, yeah. That."

"You're worried about something in your past."

"It's not really a secret." She continued to twirl the glass between her fingers. "It's public record, but yes, I'm worried. Not so much for me, but for Blake. He's built a reputable company of premier security officers. People with those credentials have to be trusted."

"What happened?"

"When I was a rookie cop—"

"You were a police officer?"

"Yes. I'd rather not go into the details, but let me just say if what happened gets out, it would jeopardize Blake's company. I'd lose my job and worse, he'd lose clients. It's taken him years to build up his security business. I can assure you since that photo of us was published, somebody has either discovered my secret, or is close to it."

"If that's true and it's already out there, then it's imperative that you become my fiancée."

She sat dumbfounded. "Excuse me?"

He cleared his throat. "For your protection, of course."

"My protection? Somehow I think it's more about yours." She clutched the glass between her fingers. "Why do I get the feeling this has been your goal since the beginning?"

A heart-stopping, boyish expression covered his face. "Because...this *has* been my goal from the beginning."

"I knew it."

"You may not be a police officer anymore, but your deductive skills are still worthy of one." He gave a slight tilt of his head as if bestowing some honor on her. "I thought it would be better to have you ease into the position. Especially since you didn't seem to like me very much."

"I don't understand. How will me being your fiancée solve anything? How will it protect Blake's company? Right now, that's all I'm concerned about."

He gave her his wonderful smile. The kind a man gives a woman making it doubly hard for said woman to refuse.

"Always thinking of others. It's one of the things I've grown to admire about you." He shifted toward her. "But you're right. The idea is purely selfish on my part."

She glanced heavenward. "Okay, I'm listening."

"It'll make the press focus on both of us, in turn, protecting Colfax Security."

"That's quite a leap," she said. "There's no guarantee of that."

"You read the article. It's all about Pricilla and me and the mystery woman who might usurp her."

"Usurp being the operative word," she said. "So, you're saying, if we're engaged, then Pricilla will have no choice but to bow out."

"Exactly. So, what do you think, mystery woman?"

"Right, mystery. Except, I won't be for much longer."

CHAPTER 11

"Thank you," Marcus said. "And since time is of the essence..." He took hold of Samantha's left hand and slipped an ornate sapphire ring on her finger.

"You were that sure of me?"

"More like, that hopeful," he said.

"Please tell me this isn't real. If anything should happen—if I should lose it—"

"You won't. Now stop fretting. We're almost there and you've just gotten engaged to a prince. You're supposed to be happy and elated."

She released a long breath and nodded.

They exited the limo and stepped out onto the red carpet which led to the entrance of the Vanderbilt Mansion in Scarsdale. Marcus laced his fingers in hers and led her along the walkway beside him, hoping his action would lead everyone around them to believe they were a couple.

He glanced at her and smiled, happy to see she smiled in return. Camera shutters clicked with a frenzy as they calmly made their way up the stone steps to the entrance. Although the slight tremor in her hand said she was anything but calm.

Once inside, he and Samantha were introduced together. He'd orchestrated this night to establish in the eye of the world that he and Samantha Keller were an item.

Marcus stayed by her side most of the evening, and when he danced with one of the other ladies in attendance his conversation, although pleasant, remained impersonal.

It was imperative that news of his relationship with Samantha spread. He would not marry Pricilla and if this most recent tactic didn't work, he'd have no choice but to further humiliate Lady Rothschild by publicly bringing an end to their relationship.

Throughout the night, he and Samantha slow-danced across the marble flooring along with the rest of the New York socialites.

"Have I told you how lovely you look this evening?" he said.

Her lips trembled when she smiled, giving him pause. Was it fair to ask her to play this game with him? Truthfully, he'd started to regret having dragged her into this mess.

He wondered how serious her mistake had been with the local police department. From what she'd said, the risk of the media finding out would hurt her boss and her. And yet she had been willing to take such a risk.

"Thank you," she said. "I'm assuming you picked the dress out for me?"

"I tried, but Eliza put up a royal fuss for the one you're wearing."

"I'll have to thank her. It's beautiful."

"You should always wear such dresses."

"I don't know. This one is rather clingy. Can't imagine where my Glock would go."

"And at this moment, imagining where your Glock would go has my full attention."

A rosy hue covered her cheeks.

"A gorgeous woman packing a pistol. Do you have any idea what such a combination does to a man?"

"Such flattery. And from a prince, no less."

"Not flattery." He brushed the back of his finger along her cheek.

"If you say so, Your Highness."

"I say so."

He pulled her close and held her as they danced and swayed to the music. It was the second time today he'd gotten to hold her with such intimacy. He knew deep down he could get used to this. The action made his heart pound and as she tucked her chin against his shoulder, he caught the scent of fresh cut flowers reminding him of the rose gardens at Sterlyn Castle.

She turned her head slightly and whispered, "How are we doing?"

He bit back a smile. "I think the press and New York's elite are getting the message that this thing between us is quite serious."

She raised her head and looked him in the eye, her gaze both sultry and sweet, her perfect, pink mouth all but asking for the inevitable.

"I wouldn't be a prince worth my kingdom if I didn't comply with a fair maid's request," he whispered.

Samantha tilted her head in confusion. He ran his gaze from her golden hair to her bare shoulders, from her slender neck, to her parted lips.

His heart pumped madly in his chest as he lowered his mouth to hers, staking his royal claim for the world to see. As he lifted his head, her eyes fluttered open, revealing a dreamy, awe-struck gaze in their depths.

Only a few seconds passed before a sweet, rosy flush covered her cheeks as she attempted to hide it. This was no game. At least not for her. It had been only a glimpse, but he'd seen it—the unmistakable spark of adoration and utter longing in Samantha Keller's eyes.

The swan had awakened.

* * *

The paparazzi swarmed Sam and the prince as they exited the limo in front of The Carlyle Hotel. Once inside, they were met with delicious quiet. They caught each other's eye and laughed, then made their way to the elevator.

Percy had hot chocolate and finger sandwiches ready for them when they entered the suite.

"You think of everything, Percy," she said. "I'm starved."

"Me too," Marcus said.

"I don't understand. Were there no refreshments at the party?"

"Oh yes," she said. "But I was way too nervous to eat a thing."

"I see. I take it your plan went off without a hitch, as you Americans like to say?"

"Yes, Percy. It did."

"Wait. Don't tell me." Sam glanced from the prince, back to Percy. "You're in on this, too?"

"I have no idea what you're talking about," Percy said, as he set the table.

Marcus turned his attention to her. "Let's get comfortable and meet back here in five."

Sam opened her mouth, then clamped it shut, realizing any objection would get nowhere with these two.

Dressed in jeans and a blue oversized sweater, Sam returned to the main sitting area to find him in jeans and a navy pullover. He stood, facing the fireplace with his back to her, so she watched him a moment longer. She'd yet to see him so ordinarily dressed and he looked amazing.

He finally turned as if sensing her presence.

"We match," he said.

"We're comfortable." She strode across the room, stopping in front of the fire. Standing next to him, she spread her hands toward the warm flames. "After a night in three-inch heels, I'm ready to relax."

"And my face is cramped from hours of smiling." He lifted his arm toward the table. "Shall we?"

"We shall."

He poured the hot chocolate into one mug then the other.

"This is a change. You, serving me."

"You deserve it. You were wonderful tonight. By now everyone in attendance will know we're an item."

"And the press? I guess they'll be weaving some fanciful story about the two of us."

"Most assuredly." He raised his mug in salute and Sam complied by lifting hers.

"All of this fanfare. Wouldn't it be easier to have a heart-to-heart with Pricilla? Can't you just tell her you're through?"

"Believe me, I've tried."

Sam shook her head.

"What?"

"You're a prince, for crying out loud. A soon to be king. Why don't you act like it?"

Marcus pressed his lips tightly together. "You think it's easy being a royal?"

"I...I wouldn't know. I'm sorry."

"No." He sighed. "You're absolutely right. I've spent most of my life being told what to do, how to think, how to act. It's exhausting."

"Poor baby." She shook her head. "No wonder you turned out so rebellious."

He raised a brow.

Her eyes widened. "Did I just say that out loud?"

"You did."

"Seems I've spoken out of turn...again."

"There have been few people brave enough to speak truth into my life. It's quite refreshing, actually."

She rested her elbows on the table. "Seriously, aren't you tired of the games? Of being manipulated by the women in your life?"

A smile played around his gorgeous mouth.

"One would think. And just what do you know about being manipulated?"

"More than I care to talk about."

He gazed at her as if he'd like to pursue the subject further. "Pricilla's one thing, but you don't know my mother. People don't tell her anything. It's yes, your Majesty, all day, all the time."

"She sounds...intimidating."

"That's one way of putting it." He bit into a sandwich and she took that as a signal to change the subject. She followed suit and pinched off a corner piece and placed it between her lips.

As she nibbled the sandwich, she eyed him. "You have so much more to offer than games."

He lifted his gaze and sat back. "I see my attempt to change the subject was conveniently lost on you."

"Well..." She hesitated and licked her lips.

"Don't stop now."

She patted her mouth with the hotel napkin. "Let's take your charity work, for instance."

"Sterlyn is involved with many charitable foundations. Between my mother and I, we make the appropriate rounds."

"Right. Appropriate. But are you really involved or is it merely for show? People can tell the difference, you know."

"You obviously have an opinion, so please enlighten me?"

"What happened to the one your father started?"

His smile faded, and he took on a curious expression. "How do you know about that?"

"I read about it once." She shrugged and took another bite of the sandwich.

"That was a long time ago. No one's mentioned it or asked me about it for years."

She ran her fingers around the back of her ear. "What happened to it?"

The prince stared into space and seemed to go someplace else. "It died...along with my father."

"But it didn't. You kept it going for several years afterward."

A strange expression covered his face. He didn't say a word, just stared at her. "How do you know all of this?"

"I told you...I must have read about it somewhere."

"We did fine work—my father and I." He stood and carefully pushed in his chair. "If you're finished, I think I'm ready to retire."

She gave a slight nod, surprised at his abrupt behavior. "Yeah. I'm pretty wiped out myself." She stood and ran her hands down the side of her jeans. "Thank you for this evening and for the sandwiches."

"My pleasure."

"Well. Good night."

"Good night."

Fifteen minutes later she climbed into the four-poster bed. She fell asleep wondering why the mention of his father's charity had caused such a strange reaction in him.

CHAPTER 12

Marcus watched Samantha leave. Curious to see who had been writing about Orphans of Ghana, he opened up his laptop. He hadn't thought about it in years and found it odd that Samantha even mentioned it. They'd barely gotten it off the ground, before his father passed away. As far as he'd been concerned, it had become lost in obscurity.

The online search revealed very little about it. The most recent date on the charity was almost fifteen years old, one year after his father died. He read the short article and except for a brief mention nothing else was said about the charity. He searched further and found another one about him and his desire to keep the foundation going in his father's memory, but that was it.

He sat back. How in the world did Samantha know about the organization? It must have been her connections to the security company. They most likely had a file on him.

He wondered what else she knew about his background. In this world of instant news there wasn't much not to know about Sterlyn and the monarchy. He liked it much better when the world focused on Princes William and Harry. Now, with Harry finally wed, the media had turned their focus on him up a notch.

He missed his father—missed his sound counsel. Most importantly, he longed for the deep friendship that had developed between them. Somewhere in his late teens, his relationship with his father had grown into one of mutual respect between two men with a similar goal and purpose.

After his father's death he'd tolerated his mother's attempts to manage him. Once he'd turned thirty, her persistence in regard to marrying Pricilla only drove him to defy her and his position. Sadly, he had become less and less like his father. And until this moment hadn't thought much about it.

He wondered what his father would think of him now. But he knew the answer. King Maxwell would not be pleased. He would have been disappointed in the prince's antics, and more importantly, in the man he'd become. Shame surged to his inner core at the thought of disappointing his dad. Had he really fallen that far away from the principles and ideals the king had taught him?

He closed out the webpage, sat back and stared across the room to the adjoining door to Samantha's suite. She'd inspired him, taken him out of his boredom, reminded him of how others saw him and the responsibility that went along with that.

Her candidness was refreshing. Because of her, he again saw his position as a gift. And that he had a responsibility to use it wisely. Once he returned to Sterlyn, he would set in motion the process of bringing back the organization—maybe even expand it to other countries in the region.

Lately he'd found himself comparing Samantha to Pricilla. The thought of Pricilla working with underprivileged children was almost comical to imagine. She would consider it dirtying her hands. But he'd no doubt that Samantha would dive right in without a second thought.

He found himself drawn to her candid, straightforward, no-nonsense behavior. Could it be possible she was becoming something more than a pawn in his game to thwart Pricilla's advances?

He shut his laptop and stood. His father would have liked Samantha. He was certain of it.

* * *

The following afternoon Prince Marcus stood next to the mayor and several city councilmen as the mayor made his final remarks welcoming the prince to the city. During his closing statement, Marcus turned his gaze on Samantha. She stood at the base of City Hall steps along with several dozen people who were in attendance.

Throughout the mayor's speech, Marcus noticed how frequently she scrolled through her phone. Whatever she was looking at had caught her attention as she seemed to check it every few seconds.

A smattering of applause peppered across the small crowd, drawing his attention back to the mayor. Marcus stepped to the podium, made a few appropriate remarks and graciously accepted the key to the city.

When the crowd dispersed, Marcus took Samantha by the hand and escorted her to the waiting car that was to take them back to the hotel for the Royal Afternoon Tea.

"What, may I ask, did you find so interesting on your phone? Was the mayor's talk that boring?"

She smiled and tipped the phone to his face. "I was checking your Instagram feed."

"I'm on Instagram?"

"Yes. I opened an account for you last night and added the hashtag—PrinceMarcusVolunteers. It's exploded on twitter, as well, and already in the high thousands. And that's just in the first few hours." She grinned. "You're on the way to a major image change, Your Highness."

He opened the limo bar and poured each of them a scotch.

"To your new image," she said, as they clicked the glasses in the air.

"And to the woman behind it."

Samantha flushed adorably at his words. He marveled at how the simplest compliment seemed to bring her such pleasure. Most likely the result of years of verbal abuse from her family.

"Thank you." She sipped the gold liquid and grimaced, then set the glass in the holder provided. "I'm not used to such compliments."

"Maybe so, but while you're with me, you can expect more." He downed the golden liquid. "We've arrived."

The tea was in full swing by the time Marcus and Samantha entered the green room at The Carlyle. It was a small affair to thank the mayor, the city council, and their families for welcoming him to the city.

Most had already taken their seat as the hotel dining staff served each table three tiers of finger sandwiches, sweets, and scones, along with an assortment of hot drinks.

"Tea or coffee, Your Highness?" a young waitress asked.

"Darjeeling for me. Samantha?"

"Darjeeling is fine, thank you."

Once the tea had been poured, he asked, "Are you looking forward to our day of shopping tomorrow?"

"That depends."

"On what?" He dipped his teaspoon into the sugar bowl. "I thought most women loved to shop."

"Most probably do."

"But not you?"

"Oh, I didn't say that." She lifted the teacup to her mouth.

"You said, 'it depends.' Depends on what?"

"On where you're planning to go. I'm assuming you'll want to hit the high-end exclusive shops like Barneys, on Madison Avenue, Giorgio's, Bergdorf Goodman."

"I'm surprised you know the store names, much less their locations."

"Oh, I did my homework, remember? The fashion magazines you so kindly supplied for my preparation?"

He couldn't help but smile. "Touché, Miss Keller."

"I'm sure these stores and boutiques will be fitting establishments providing an ample array of gifts for your mother, your friends, Percy, Pricilla—"

"Stop right there." He eyed her for a moment. "I chose this day for you. One, on the assumption that most women like to shop and two, on the assumption that since I was having you work, day and night, I thought you'd like some time to Christmas shop...for your family and friends."

"Oh." She gazed at him in surprise. "How thoughtful of you. In that case, I look forward to it."

CHAPTER 13

The following morning, Sam entered the suite and found Percy in the middle of Solitaire.

"So. You're a card player."

"During my down time, yes. I find it relaxes me."

"Where's Marcus?" She strode across the room.

"He had to run out for a while. Would you like to play a quick game of cards while you wait?"

"I thought you'd never ask." She tossed her handbag on the floor and took the seat across from him while he shuffled the deck.

"Poker all right with you?"

"Sure."

She collected her cards from the table. As she spread them through her fingers, she glanced at the pensive face of the prince's man. What she'd first thought stoic and reserved now looked kind and fatherly. He was a man of insight, and his concern touched her. She thought of her own father, who was a lot like the man sitting across from her with his gentle and quiet spirit. She missed her dad terribly and knew if he'd lived, her life would have turned out so differently. She certainly wouldn't be facing such dire financial difficulties.

"Where are you, Miss Samantha? It's your move."

"Oh. Sorry." She offered a smile.

"Are you all right? You seem preoccupied."

"You don't miss much, do you, Percy?"

"It is my job not to, especially when it comes to the prince."

She nodded, threw down two cards, then drew two more from the deck. As much as she'd like to, it would be totally inappropriate to discuss her financial situation with the man.

"You and Marcus seem close. At least on the surface."

"As close as monarch and servant are allowed."

"Forgive me for saying so, but I don't think the prince sees you as a servant. I've noticed how he sometimes even defers to your judgment."

"Only since his father passed away."

She laid down her hand. Two queens and three sevens.

A slight smile touched Percy's lips as he laid down his cards. "Good, but not good enough, I'm afraid."

"A royal flush," she said. "Nice."

"Who taught you to play?" he asked.

"My father."

"Are you two close?" he asked, as he gathered up the deck.

"We were. He died when I was eleven."

"I'm very sorry."

She shrugged. "It's all right."

"The prince wasn't much older when he lost his."

"We have that in common."

He stood. "Would you like refreshment before the next hand?"

She nodded.

A few minutes later he placed two glasses of lemonade on the table with a small plate of cookies.

She took a long drink and eyed the middle-aged man in front of her. He had to be a wealth of knowledge regarding the prince. There was so much she wished to know. Things far beyond what the tabloids offered. Maybe this would be a good time for her to ask a few questions.

"There's something I don't understand," she said.

Percy gave her his full attention.

"As the next in line for the throne, doesn't he have any say in who he marries?"

"Three hundred years of protocol is difficult to ignore. Besides, he has the people of Sterlyn to consider." He drew a card from the deck. "Although a small country, we are a proud people, steeped in tradition, and we love our monarchy.

"That said, I happen to agree with you. Forcing one into marriage, even for the noblest of reasons, is never a good idea."

Percy glanced at her hands. "I can't help but notice how you favor your uh...engagement ring."

Her fingers stilled, and she eyed her left hand. "So, did you two hatch-up this insanity together?"

His sudden, easy smile was answer enough.

She'd been twisting and turning the beautiful stone ever since the prince slid it on her finger. "I hate deceiving people. And if Marcus would just stand up for his rights, this wouldn't be necessary."

"I'm afraid it's not that simple. Imagine being groomed from birth for one thing—one job—without being given the choice for any other. No matter where your heart may take you, you know you cannot go there.

"Of course, he could simply quit, leave the country, disavow the throne and all that goes with it. But what kind of man would he be? How could he live with himself knowing there were no other heirs to take his place?"

"He would never do that. And I'm not suggesting that he should." She spread out her hands. "I just hate to see him reduced to more games."

"I agree. There is also a set of rules for a man in my position and it's not my place to instruct him. There's a strong-spirited man inside of him and maybe you're just the woman to bring that person to the surface."

Percy gazed at her with a look that challenged. "I believe it's your turn to deal."

As he handed her the deck, she wondered if there was a deeper message in his words.

"How about a nice hand of Scabby Queen?" he said.

"I'm sorry. What?"

"I believe you Americans call it, Old Maid. Except in this instance the queen of clubs—the scabby queen, is the old maid."

* * *

Marcus entered the suite in time to see Samantha crowing over an apparent win at cards and Percy shaking his head as if in defeat. Samantha whispered something across the table, and Percy gave a hearty laugh.

"Don't you two look chummy." Their heads turned simultaneously and the look of merriment on his betrothed's face stopped him mid-stride. All laughter and smiles—she was radiant.

He tried to imagine Pricilla laughing and joking with Percy and knew she would never put herself in a subservient position to those she considered beneath her station. The joyless state of affairs with her as mistress of Sterlyn Castle loomed to the forefront of his mind. He could not let that happen.

"Your highness, we didn't hear you come in." Percy started to stand.

"Stay seated, Percy, and enjoy your card game."

"And have her beating me again? No thank you."

Percy gathered up the cards as Samantha downed the rest of her lemonade.

"And don't you look unusually casual," she said.

"It's what one wears on their morning jog."

"If you ran in Central Park, I hope you took your security detail with you."

"Don't worry. I did."

Truthfully, he liked the way she worried about him. Although he didn't need her protection, her instincts to do so touched him.

"I have a surprise for you," she said.

"Wonderful, I like surprises."

"Percy, cancel whatever he has on his agenda today," Samantha said.

Percy lifted a brow and turned his attention to the prince.

"You heard the lady."

Percy dipped his head and left.

Samantha crossed the room and pulled a wool hat and sunglasses from her purse. She held them up. "Your disguise."

She secured the toboggan over his head, slipped the glasses over his nose, then stepped back. "Perfect. No one will recognize you in that. Now put on your warm coat and let's go."

Marcus retrieved his coat then waited while Samantha slipped into her wool jacket. After they took the lift to the lobby, Samantha took his hand and led him through the kitchen.

"We're going out the back." She checked her phone as they exited the building. "I've called an Uber, and it'll be here in two minutes."

The car pulled up right on time and they climbed in.

"Where are we going?"

"You'll see."

The Uber driver dropped them off at Rockefeller Center.

"I'm assuming you know how to ice skate," she said.

"You assume correctly."

Once their skates were on and laced up, Samantha took his hand and stepped out onto the ice. She pulled him along, sliding expertly over the frozen rink.

"I'd almost forgotten how much I love this," he said. "Thank you."

"You're welcome. Ever since I can remember, my dad and I started the Christmas season right here."

"You miss him, don't you?"

"Every day."

"Thank you for allowing me to be a part of your tradition."

A thoughtful smile curved her mouth. "I hadn't thought of it like that, but you're right. It's time I got back to some of my traditions."

In that moment her blue eyes were full of life, pain, and unquenchable warmth. She opened her mouth to speak, then thought better of it and glanced down. She swallowed and looked up.

"You handle yourself well on the ice," she said.

Whatever she'd been about to say, wasn't that. At times Samantha Keller was an open book, and at others, a mystery. Heaven help him, it was the mystery he longed to know.

"You're not so bad yourself."

As they made the turn side by side, he took hold of her hand and spun her around. The momentum caught her off guard. He caught her to his chest to steady her.

"Sorry about that," he said. "Next time I'll warn you."

Arms around his neck, she clung to him. "Good, because I'd hate to end up on my rear end."

She started to let go of him. "No, don't. I like you here."

Face to face, she gazed up at him. He loved the way her blue eyes sparkled when she was happy. How, at this moment, her slightly open mouth begged to be kissed. The cold air brought a rosy hue to her cheeks. A snowflake touched her face, then another. He lifted a finger and brushed the wet from her cheek.

This past week, Samantha had blossomed like a flower in spring. He couldn't deny his growing attraction to her. But not knowing where this thing between them would lead, he knew he should take it slow.

But certainly, one little kiss right here on the ice wouldn't hurt. Just. One. Kiss...

And as if she'd read his thoughts, she arched forward as he lowered his mouth to hers. His kiss was brief and sweet, and he savored every second.

When he lifted his head, her glowing eyes searched his face. The last thing he wanted was to hurt her. He'd seen the affection in her gaze when he'd caught her staring at him.

As Prince of Sterlyn he'd grown used to his share of second glances and female crushes. But not until Samantha had he experienced his own. For the feelings she stirred within his heart were definitely crush-worthy. He thought about her constantly and could hardly wait for each day with her.

It was time he learned more about her. Percy's request to Blake St. John regarding Samantha resulted in little information. Something about a privacy act and her record being confidential.

"How about something to drink?" he said.

She nodded. "They have the best hot cocoa here."

"Sounds good."

* * *

As much as she tried, Sam could not stop thinking about that sweet, delicious kiss. She could tell he'd wanted to. Heck, *she'd* wanted to. And pretty much asked for it. Then his abrupt suggestion they stop for a drink had her rethinking the whole thing.

It wasn't like they were trying to impress the media. He was in disguise. So, it must have been the real deal.

Her mind continued in this vein as they removed their skates and took their seats in the snack area. Getting off the ice and out of the snow should help get her mind onto something else.

While Marcus ordered the hot chocolate, she checked Instagram.

"Oh my gosh. You have one hundred thousand followers on Instagram." She held her phone to his face. "Let me check Twitter." She scrolled the screen with her thumb. "Twenty-five thousand. Not as many, but still really good. So, what do you think?"

"I haven't checked my phone in days. But those numbers sound amazing."

"Look, I know you have hundreds of thousands of followers, but this has to do with your hashtag. The new you, if you will. You should go on sometime and read a few of the comments." She sat up straight. "I think you'll be impressed."

"I have to confess I tend to stay away from social media. There're just as many negative things said about me as positive. I prefer not to read them."

The waiter placed two mugs of hot chocolate and a small bowl of marshmallow cream in front of them.

"How about I share some of the good ones with you sometime?"

"I'll wait with bated breath." His warm eyes met her blue ones.

"Your sarcasm has been noted, Your Highness."

Sam spooned the sweet confection into her cocoa. "Now that that's settled, tell me about your father?" She blew across the top of the mug. "I don't know that much about him, only what I've read."

"You seem to have *read* a lot about us."

Heat flushed her cheeks, and she glanced at her cocoa, hoping to hide her discomfort. She wondered how long she'd be able to keep her knowledge of him from coming out.

"I have read a lot about you." She cleared her throat. "Research. I always research my clients. Colfax provides us with background information for each job we take." She took a hasty sip of cocoa, almost scalding her tongue.

She'd read everything about the prince she could get her hands on since she was eleven. Not that it really mattered, but if he found out she'd been crushing on him all those years ago, she'd be embarrassed beyond belief.

It was obvious from his words that he'd started to question where she'd gotten her information about him. Her pat answer that she'd 'read it somewhere' was getting old. Hopefully her explanation would put his curiosity to rest.

He rested his forearms on the edge of the table. "My father was known as the people's king. Which I'm sure you've learned from your extensive reading on the subject."

His eyes held an engaging twinkle that had her heart beating double-time.

"He was genuine, the real deal and raised me to be the same. Though, I have to admit, the past several years, I've failed in that respect. But thanks to an opinionated young woman, I'm working on rectifying that."

"Always happy to be of service." She smiled, taking a sip of cocoa.

He cradled his mug in his hands, a pensive expression on his handsome face. "He mingled with the working man. Whether it was at the local pubs, or to simply hunt and fish alongside them. He was unique in that respect. Even that side of him drove my mother crazy. He was a great ruler. No one rivaled his wisdom and compassion—his humanity. When he died, all of Sterlyn mourned."

"I'm sorry. I know how painful it is to lose one's father."

He nodded. "At the time, no one expected me to fill his shoes, but I still felt the weight of it."

"You were a teenager. How could you?"

He eyed her from across the Formica top. "You would have liked him and he you."

She placed her elbows on the table and rested her chin in her hands. "Tell me about the charity you and he started? Why orphans?"

"He wanted to instill in me that with privilege comes great responsibility. I think he chose to work with children because I was a child, and he thought it would help me to identify with them."

"Makes sense."

"After my father's death I tried to keep it going, but my mother had other plans. She felt differently, believing in the importance of an exemplary lifestyle, keeping oneself above the fray of the mundane."

"Which was not at all like your father."

"Exactly. Protocol was far more important to her. She established new traditions to set an example for those in the kingdom. Before I knew it, I'd let others manage the charity resulting in me having less and less input in its running, until it became something other than what my father and I had started."

"You know, I owe you an apology. You've done so much for so many people."

"Thank you, but that's not what you said a few days ago. Why the change of heart?"

"My limited world cannot compare with a kingdom, a country. I judged you by my own standards and that's just not fair."

He didn't speak a word—didn't have to. His warm, brown-eyed gaze said it all.

"Now that I've bared my soul, I'd like to hear more about you," he said.

"Compared to yours, my life has been pretty dull," she said.

"How have you survived living with Katherine and Tiffany?"

"One day at a time." She grinned. "Seriously, though, they depend on my income or I would have asked them to leave a long time ago." She shook her head causing a golden strand to fall over her forehead. She pushed it off her face, tucking it behind her ear.

"You're independent and resilient. You're a fighter. I admire that in you."

"Thanks, but some days I feel trapped, like no matter what I do, I can't get ahead. Not that you would know anything about that."

"Not to the same degree, but I get it. The pressure to marry Pricilla has hung over my head for years."

She spooned another dollop of marshmallow cream into her mug, then took a sip. "Since my father's death I've spent most of my days trying to survive in a household where love was absent."

"I take it, Katherine was the only mother you ever knew."

"Yes, and I've spent many years trying to win her approval." She fingered the rim of her mug. "As an adult I've come to accept my lot. It's been my norm for over ten years now. Sounds lame, I know. But it's not without its perks."

"How so?"

"I discovered the act of giving, without expecting anything in return, brought more than I could ever have imagined. A special blessing that far outweighed any hatefulness on their part.

"Eventually, I began to pity them, and still do." She shrugged. "Sure, I would've loved to have had their affection, but it wasn't to be."

"But you've found love from other quarters, like the residents at Oakland Manor. I've seen how you work with them and how much they adore you. You're open, honest, and kind-hearted."

Moved by his thoughtful words, she gazed at him, doing her best not to reveal her true feelings where he was concerned. Kind words or not, she knew their make-believe world was nothing but a game to thwart Lady Pricilla's pursuit. He'd made that perfectly clear.

Her gaze dropped to his perfect mouth and that sweet kiss on the ice. The notion that her ordinary existence could become extraordinary because of Marcus was simply a girlhood dream—a fantasy. And foolish to think he could ever be interested in her at all.

CHAPTER 14

The following morning, Sam left The Carlyle early to check on Katherine. She had little confidence in Tiffany's verbal commitment to take care of her mother as she'd promised.

The house was quiet when she entered. She stopped by the kitchen desk and scooped up the mail. Most of it was junk except for one or two items. There were two from the bank, both addressed to Katherine. She checked the date on the envelope. They were from three months ago.

Not one to open someone else's mail, she tapped the letters on her left hand and glanced around the kitchen. With Katherine's mental state and the fact that they hadn't been opened, she tore into the first one.

It was a late notice on the second mortgage her stepmother had taken out several months ago. With a slight tightening in her chest, she opened the second letter. A final notice from the bank, this time with late fees attached.

Final notice?

Her heart sank. How was this possible? Every two weeks, she'd faithfully deposited her checks into the household account. She'd even set up automatic withdrawal with the bank to keep something like this from happening.

As she stared at the notice, Tiffany slumped into the kitchen dressed in her nightgown and furry slippers. She stopped mid-stride, then crossed the ceramic tile floor to the coffee pot. "I see you're wearing your usual scowl. What did mother and I do wrong, now?"

Sam squeezed her eyes tightly shut, then shoved the bank letter under Tiff's nose.

"If you would occasionally take some responsibility for your mother and the bills, it would be most appreciated. What the heck happened here?"

Tiffany squinted over the paper in Sam's hands. "What is it?"

"Past due notices from the bank. We're almost three months behind on the mortgage payment. How is this possible?"

Tiffany shrugged as a satin strap fell from her left shoulder. She turned, coffee mug in hand, and strolled into the next room. Sam followed.

"Well?"

"I may have cashed a few checks."

"A few?"

"And ran up my credit card a bit," Tiffany added.

Sam shook her head in amazement. "At the risk of losing our home? A roof over our heads? Have you no thought for your mother?"

"Relax. It's only a couple of months." She blew over the top of the mug and took a hesitant sip. "I'm sure you'll think of something. You always do." She slumped into one of the club chairs.

"I don't make enough money to cover this. Especially with the added late fees."

Tiffany's eyes widened. "Oh my god."

"What is it? What's wrong?"

"Your ring. You're engaged?"

Sam glanced at her left hand. She'd forgotten to slip it off before she came home. She couldn't very well tell Tiff it was all a sham, a ruse.

Tiff shot from the chair, then snatched up Sam's hand. She didn't say a word. Her heaving chest and the darts flying from her glacial stare said it all.

Sam yanked her hand from Tiffany's grasp. "Whether I'm engaged or not has nothing to do with the problem at hand. I cannot take care of all three of us without some help. The least you could do is stop spending the money I earn. Have you no self-respect?"

"Apparently not." She took a swig of her coffee. "Cold." She grimaced and went back into the kitchen.

For a long moment, Sam stared after her, then glanced at the notice now crushed in her fist. She'd go to the bank—transfer some money from her savings. She was pretty sure she had enough to cover at least two months.

Seconds later she heard activity from the kitchen. It was Katherine. She turned as Sam entered.

"Good morning. Are you here for long? Don't you have a job away from here?" She gazed at Sam with clear, questioning innocence. A look Sam noticed grew more and more frequent as the weeks went by.

"No. Not for long. I just came by to check on you and to get my mail."

She stepped closer and placed her hand on Katherine's shoulder. "How are you feeling today?"

"Right as rain." She smiled.

Sam glanced at the crumpled notice in her palm and wondered if she should ask Katherine about it. "I'm glad to hear it."

Her stepmother grabbed a bowl from the cabinet, then sat at the table and prepared her simple breakfast of toast and cereal.

"I found the letters from the bank," Sam said. "The past due notices." She stood hovering over Katherine as the woman spooned milk and cereal into her mouth. As Katherine chewed, Sam wondered if she'd heard her.

"I meant to tell you, but I forgot," Katherine said.

"What do you mean? How could you have known? I just now opened the letters."

"There're more."

Sam stared unblinking. She shot a quick glance toward Tiffany before focusing again on her stepmom. "How...how many?"

"They started coming a couple of months after I took out the second mortgage. Four, maybe five. I lost count." She became agitated. "I told Tiffany to tell you."

Sam's heart lurched, and her mind reeled. She stared at Tiffany, who shrugged and focused on her coffee. Sam stood, rooted to the floor, glancing from one Step to the other. Anything else she may have said would have only fallen on deaf, uninterested ears.

From the time she'd been old enough to get a job, she'd been the responsible one. Through her childhood she'd trusted in Katherine's ability to manage her father's estate. It wasn't until she became an adult that she realized money was tight and that her income would now be essential to meet the needs of the household.

For years she'd watched her Steps go through the money he'd left behind and watched as they grew more and more dependent on her income to make ends meet.

With her stomach in knots, she left the house. An hour later, she sat across from their family banker, Clark Meyers.

"I'm sorry, Samantha, but there's only enough in your savings to cover the past three months."

"Which will deplete my savings."

He nodded. "Your stepmother is still behind on another one and that's not counting this month's, which will come due on the thirty-first." He hesitated and glanced down as if dreading his next words. "If you can't make the payments, your loan will go into default. Do you understand what that means?"

She nodded as panic rioted within her. "The bank will have to sell the property."

CHAPTER 15

Sam stood by one of the crystal punch bowls stationed between two large Corinthian columns to the right of the large Christmas tree. The scent of fresh pine mingled with the smell of beef tenderloin, hot bread and sugary sweets.

Smiling her thanks to the server, she stepped right and positioned herself near a Queen Anne loveseat.

She took a sip of the champagne punch and glanced around the glittering, ornate space. She'd never seen so many beautifully dressed women. Men in their black tuxedos made the perfect complement to the ladies' festive evening gowns. The entire scene played-out like a fairy tale.

As she gazed around the elegant room, she spotted a familiar dress, blinked, and tilted her head left for a closer look. The woman wearing it was partially hidden behind a column wrapped in sparkly red ribbon.

Seconds later, the woman stepped right, giving Samantha a perfect view of her profile. Her heart sank.

Tiffany stood chatting as only Tiff could do—with animation and gaiety. Sam had never known her not to be the life of any party she'd attended. In that moment, Tiff turned to face Sam from across the room. She winked, then turned back to the gentleman at her side.

On closer look, she saw the man was none other than Mr. Yachtsman himself, Jason Osborne. All Sam could do was stare. How in the world did he and Tiffany get an invitation to this event? She'd personally seen the guest list only a few days ago, and neither one had been on it, and she had insisted she be informed if anyone was added in the meantime.

She downed the rest of the punch. Having forgotten it had been spiked, she sputtered and gasped for air. Taking a second to recover, she set the glass on a nearby tray and ran her hands down the length of her hips. Knowing she couldn't very well ignore her stepsister, she made her way around the edges of the ballroom. A guest had claimed Osborne's attention when she reached Tiff's side.

"Well, hello, Stepsister," Tiffany said.

"Tiffany. Isn't that my mother's dress?"

"Relax, it's not like I've stolen it." Tiff glanced down at the flowing fabric. "It's been stuffed at the back of your closet for eons, so I figured you wouldn't mind if I wore it."

Truthfully, she didn't mind. It was more the shock of seeing it on her at this gala, than anything else. With the subject of the dress out of the way, she pulled Tiffany aside. "What are you doing here?"

"You think you're the only one with connections to the royal family?"

"What connections could you possibly have? What are you up to?"

"Nothing...at the moment." Tiffany flashed a smile, took a step away from her, then looped her arm underneath the man's standing beside her. "Jason, this is my stepsister, Samantha Keller."

"It's a pleasure," he said, shaking Sam's hand.

"Jason is an acquaintance of Lady Pricilla Rothschild, so he snagged an invite to the prince's ball. Isn't that wonderful?"

Sam stared, mouth gaping. "It certainly is."

Marcus appeared in Sam's line of vision and, when she caught his eye, she quickly glanced away. The last thing she wanted was for him to meet Tiffany. But no sooner had she thought it than he strode across the room, making his way to her side.

He gently touched her back, smiled at her, then turned his attention to Tiffany and Jason. "Good evening. I don't believe we've met." Marcus stuck out his hand, and Jason clasped it.

"Jason Osborne, and this is Tiffany Draper."

Tiffany extended her hand to Marcus. "Sam's step-sister."

Marcus raised a brow and glanced from Tiffany to Sam.

Sam forced a smile and nodded. "That she is. And I believe you met her mother the other day."

He gave his attention back to Tiffany. "So, you're the daughter of that...lovely woman?"

Tiffany tilted her head to the side and looked confused, before smiling brightly. "Sam, you should've told us about the prince." Tiffany fluttered her false eyelashes and glanced coyly at Marcus. "Keeping a secret is not like our Sam."

* * *

Marcus gave a slight bow, then glanced from one woman to the other. The tension between these step siblings could be sliced in two with the king's sword. If this had been the eighteenth-century, Tiffany would have smacked Samantha's knuckles with a fan for her impertinence.

Tiffany was indeed a beguiling creature, and it was evident there had been competition between the two over the years. He could certainly see how her natural beauty could lead to competition between the two.

Poor little Samantha. Between Mrs. Keller's hateful rhetoric and Tiffany's exceptional good looks, was it any wonder Samantha had come to feel inferior?

He caught the undeniable flicker of pain in Samantha's eyes before she bravely lifted her chin and smiled.

"Nice meeting you, Jason," she said. "Enjoy the evening." She turned to Marcus. "Your Highness," Sam placed her hand on his arm, "I believe this next dance belongs to me."

Even though she smiled cordially, her intense stare pleaded.

"So, it does." He turned toward the other two. "If you'll excuse us."

Without taking his eyes off her, he escorted Samantha to the dance floor.

Shoulders back, head high, she followed him with beauty and grace befitting a woman of means. Except she wasn't a woman of means, but a working girl from a place called Queens.

So far, their ruse seemed to be working. The questioning glances from the guests would turn into actual questions from the media, both here and abroad.

Although her lips spread with a glorious smile, it faded ever so slightly as he took her in his arms.

As he gazed at her, a soft mist filled her eyes as if she fought to hold back tears. He tipped her chin, giving her no other choice but to look at him. She smiled and nodded signaling all was well, even though he knew it wasn't.

She was lovely and brave and truly beautiful. He could tell it had pained her to find her stepsister here, a sting that went far deeper than the simple crashing of a party. He determined, then and there, to find out how Jason Osborne had acquired an invitation to this event.

At that moment, Pricilla appeared from behind the gilded column to stand next to Tiffany and her date. Of course. He should have known. The entire scene had the mark of Pricilla's conniving influence. From the looks of the chummy trio it was obvious Pricilla knew Osborne. Which shouldn't have surprised him as her connections to New York City's elite had been well established for many years through her family's international investments.

Sorry Pricilla, but you've over-stepped this time.

* * *

Leave it to Tiffany to spoil even this. On the surface, the prince hadn't fallen for her coquettish ways. But Sam wasn't about to test that. Another few minutes in her company and who knows what could have happened.

Tiff had a way with the opposite sex. Sam had witnessed her man-trap skills on more than one occasion. Coaxing her way into many a man's heart only to drop them for another higher up on the rich and famous ladder.

And the prince was both rich and famous.

She glanced up to find the prince's dreamy eyes focused on her. Even though they held a smile, they also asked a million questions. Questions she didn't wish to answer. But the prince was nothing if not tenacious and before this night was over, he'd have her spilling everything. A week ago, she'd have told him to mind his own business, but now, she actually longed to share her cares with someone—more specifically, with him.

Somehow her feet kept on moving in step with his. She had no idea if it was the atmosphere, the small orchestra or simply Marcus himself, but she found herself wanting to tell him her entire life's story and to discover his. What she'd gleaned from the tabloids and Percy's small talk just wasn't enough.

If someone had told her she'd be dancing in the arms of a prince, dressed in the finest gown she'd ever seen, and feeling safer than she had in many years, she'd have said they were smoking something illegal.

A heady sensation filled her, as if all her senses had suddenly awakened. She decided then and there to enjoy the moment—the magnificent music and the intimacy of the waltz.

Tiffany in the wings was certainly cause for alarm. Sam knew her Step did nothing without an ulterior motive, especially when it came to her. She stood, waiting for the ax to fall as she tried to figure out how Tiff could even be here.

A sick sensation pooled in the pit of her stomach. The same feeling she'd experienced when they told her she'd failed the blood test. Alarm, disbelief, shock. But Sam refused to allow Tiffany to ruin what could possibly be her last evening with the prince.

She took pleasure in the slight pressure of his hand at her lower back as he deftly guided her across the dance floor. And her heart raced at the thought of what it would be like to be truly and irrevocably his.

She would call on her girlhood imagination and enjoy this evening. If she'd learned anything in life, it was that you only had the moment you were in. Nothing else mattered.

A fool's dream. She knew that, and yet...

She gulped, pushed down the giddy sensation and focused her attention on the top button on his crisp, white shirt. The prince was experienced in love and women, and it wouldn't do to let him see the affect he was having on her. She had a job to do. Best leave it at that.

She lifted her gaze in time to see him level a glance at someone else in the room. When the glance turned into a lingering stare Sam instinctively knew who'd caught his attention. Turning her head slightly she caught her stepsister's syrupy, red-lipped smile.

Her heart sank. She glanced back at the prince to find his gaze now on her —a slight frown creasing his handsome brow.

Oh gosh. There it was... The thing she'd most dreaded. She'd experienced it all before and more times than she cared to remember. The comparisons. The, how could these two sisters be from the same family, expression? Then, the ah-ha moment, followed by the pitying smile, when they learned the sisters were not really blood related at all.

How many times, in her teenage dreams, had she gazed at his poster while longing for him to look at her with the same fervor and intensity he'd just bestowed on Tiffany.

As she pushed back the humiliation, her gaze locked on that excruciatingly close broad shoulder mere inches from her forehead. If only she could close her eyes and rest her cheek right there—tucked against his chest—secure in his arms.

If only...

But this relationship thing was all a game, a ruse, a disguise for the gawkers and onlookers.

She blinked back the sudden rush of tears and kept her head where it belonged. Regal and upright as he'd taught her. As if she hadn't a care in the world.

CHAPTER 16

As the evening progressed, Marcus searched for an opportunity to speak to Pricilla. He spotted her coming from behind the long brocade curtain near one of the bay windows overlooking the hotel courtyard. He skirted his way around and grabbed hold of her arm before she could step away.

"My, aren't we aggressive this evening." Her smile held an unpleasant twist. "Careful darling, or you might create a scene."

"I don't know what game you're playing but it's not going to work. What are you doing here?"

"As your betrothed, I have every right to be here."

"A verbal agreement between well-meaning parents does not constitute a betrothal, or an engagement, or anything else. And in case you've missed seeing it, I've placed a ring on Samantha Keller's left hand."

Her smile vanished. "I will not lose you to some American nobody."

"You have to already have something in order to lose it. Samantha Keller has more in her character to be a princess than you've ever displayed. I will never marry you, Pricilla. I'm giving you twenty-four hours to break it off. It's your opportunity to save face. Use whatever excuse you'd like. I really don't care."

"And if I refuse?"

"I find it hard to believe you'd so callously risk the long-standing and deep friendship between our families."

The venomous stare she bestowed on him spoke volumes. "I could say the same to you."

"And it's my sincere hope it doesn't come to that," he said.

"Do you actually think your mother will accept Samantha Keller as the next Princes of Sterlyn?"

"What my mother accepts has nothing to do with you."

Tiffany appeared as if on cue—as if her entrance had been choreographed.

"Just the person I wanted to see." Pricilla purred, linking her arm with Tiffany's. "Tell me about your delightful stepsister. I'm anxious to learn everything about her. It's not just anyone who can capture the attention of our prince here." She glanced slyly at him, no doubt to make absolutely certain he'd heard her.

With that, the two women turned their backs to him and strolled off. He had no doubt Tiffany was already filling Pricilla's ears with gossip.

As he stepped back into the ballroom, he spotted Samantha at the far wall sitting next to an elderly woman. Her rapt attention to the lady was not lost on him. He loved that about her. How she attended to the woman's every word. He'd witnessed it with the residents at Oakland Manor, and with her thoughtful attention to Percy.

As she chatted with the lady, she seemed completely devoid of her earlier distress in having discovered her stepsister in attendance. He knew there was something in Samantha's past that worried her. And high time, he discovered just what that something was.

Pricilla would certainly find out and use it against Samantha. And that would never do.

He reached Samantha's side just as the elderly woman turned her attention to a portly gentleman seated to her right. He bowed slightly, and acknowledged the elderly couple, then turned to Sam. "Would you care to dance?"

"I'd love to." She stood and placed her hand in his.

He led her to the dance floor and took her in his arms. He enjoyed his brief moments of holding her close, and as dancing was his only outlet, he took full advantage of it. If she'd been taller, they would have danced cheek-to-cheek.

Since the top of her head barely reached his chin, she had to tilt her head back to look at him. He'd wanted her to relax against him, place her head against his shoulder, but she spoke, instead.

"What's on your mind, Prince?"

The smile in her voice elicited one of his own as he gazed down at her upturned face. She was beautiful. Soft tendrils framed her forehead and her clear blue eyes mirrored the jewel of the same color that hung at the hollow of her neck.

He wondered if he should actually tell her what he'd been thinking. That he'd confronted Pricilla, told her he'd never marry her. And that he'd attributed his courage to do so at Samantha's door? Should he tell her of her stepsister's part in the discussion? That the two women were at this moment most likely plotting Samantha's demise?

"You," he said.

Samantha angled her head in confusion.

"I'm thinking of you."

Her cheeks flushed a pretty pink, and she lowered her gaze to his bowtie. Obviously, she hadn't expected that. He found her sudden shyness interesting and adorable. Samantha who was never at a loss for words. At least when it came to him.

The change in her had been remarkable. He'd like to have taken credit for it but knew the credit was all hers. She'd always been a swan living amongst ducks. And whatever happened after their time together, he hoped she'd at least come to recognize that.

As they continued to dance to the slow rhythm, he realized just how much he liked holding her close. He appreciated the ease in which they'd conversed. Adding her to the top of the list as one of the few people who needn't stand on ceremony with him.

From the beginning she made it clear by her words and actions that she was his equal. He liked and respected that...and her. She'd brought out the best in him and had accomplished something no other woman to date had done. She'd captured his heart.

Chapter 17

A shrill ring penetrated Sam's sleepy brain as her right hand fumbled to grab the cell phone. She clasped it between her fingers and lifted it to her cheek.

"Hello," she said, her voice groggy.

"I want you in my office. Now."

"Chief? What's wrong?" Her head spun from the wine, the dancing, and Tiffany's unwelcomed presence at the party. She blinked and sat up.

"Be here, ready to explain yourself in one hour."

Before she could say another word, he'd hung up. She placed the phone on her bedside table and threw off the bed covers. Fully awake now, she took a moment to gather her thoughts. Something bad must have happened for Blake to call her in on the carpet.

His indignation rang in her ears as she swung her feet to the floor. Her heart sank as she thought of a similar call she'd received a few years ago from the New York Police Department.

She could identify a death knell when she heard one.

Blake was on the phone as she entered his office. He waved her to the chair opposite his desk. Keeping her eyes on him, she sat and waited. When he'd hung up, he didn't say a word, just stood looking down at her with a sober expression.

"You've made the paper...again." He tossed the *New York Times* on the desk in front of her, then stuffed his hands into his pockets.

She gazed at the black and white print. "I don't see anything here that—"

He leaned forward and flipped the newspaper over. She lowered her head and read.

'Colfax Security Hires Former NYPD Officer Who Failed Drug Test.'

She lifted her hand to the side of her neck. As she scanned the article, the failed drug test, the firing, and the humiliation all rushed back as if it had happened yesterday.

"And that's not all." Blake tossed the *New York Post,* the *am New York,* and *Metro New York* in front of her.

"*Metro New York*. Never heard of it," she said.

"Maybe you haven't, but one-hundred cities across Europe, North and South America *and* Asia certainly have."

"I...I don't understand. I don't know how—"

"Do you really think you could be the Prince of Sterlyn's latest, and the media not find out everything they can about you?"

"You have no right to lay this at my door. Supplying me with fashion magazines for the job. You had to have known something like this would happen."

At least he had the decency to look sheepish. But unfortunately for her it only lasted a second. He pressed his fingers to his forehead and sat.

"I didn't know," he said. "I thought the magazines were to aid you in the proper dress for the assignment. I thought you'd be part of his security. And I never imagined you'd become his latest item."

"I'm sorry, sir."

"So am I. The article puts my company in a very bad light for having hired you. Not only locally but around the world. I have no choice but to let you go."

"I know." She stood. "I'll resign. No. You need to fire me."

Blake's face became a study in confusion.

"For the optics, sir. You need to do whatever it takes to save Colfax."

"Optics aside, I feel badly about it, but my clients have to have the trust of the company and the officers in it."

"I know. I've undermined Colfax Security and put your reputation at stake. I'll clear out my desk."

Samantha left the building carrying her personal items in a cardboard box. She'd have to get her things at the hotel, as well. Most likely Blake had already informed the prince of her firing and had wasted no time in sending a replacement.

Thirty minutes later, she arrived at her suite to find Marcus waiting for her.

"I guess you've heard what happened—seen the article in the paper, by now."

"I have. Are you all right?"

She lowered her gaze. "Not really."

She stepped to pass him, and he took hold of her arm. "Samantha."

She swung toward him. "It's all right. I've been here before. I just came for my things. Blake should be sending someone else to take my place. I know you put a lot of work into my...training. I'm sorry you had to waste your time."

"Samantha Keller. I would never describe my time spent with you as a waste. On the contrary. My time with you has been one of the most entertaining and enlightening experiences of my life."

"Well, I'm happy to have been able to amuse you, but I need to go."

She twisted away from his grasp, crossed the room, then began tossing her things into her suitcase.

"As much as I appreciate this brave front of yours, have you forgotten we are engaged?"

For a second her hand stilled on a yellow blouse. She tugged the Sapphire ring from her left hand, then held it toward him. "Now, we're not."

He folded his arms and gazed down at her. "I refuse to take it back."

Her lips parted and her jaw fell in the most appealing manner. He watched as her mind seemed to search for what to say next.

"Well, that's just ridiculous. Take the darn ring."

"No."

"Fine." She placed it on the bedside table and proceeded to finish her packing.

"Look. I could care less about what Blake thinks. Your past and that article has nothing to do with me. You and I had a deal."

She spun back around. "Seriously? You're actually making this about you?"

Jaw clenched, he ran his hand around the back of his neck.

"The deal is off," she said.

"I never would have thought you a quitter."

"I'm not. But keeping me in the public eye will further hurt Blake and Colfax. I can't do that. I *won't* do that."

He took her hand in his. "Tell me your side of the story."

"You won't leave this alone, will you?" Brow furrowed, she plopped down on the edge of the bed.

He gently squeezed her hand. "Please."

"I failed a drug test. That's it."

She glanced at him to gage his reaction, but he continued to look at her with the same interest and concern as before.

"As a result, I lost my job with the NYPD. It was all over the news." She pressed her fingers to her forehead. "All I ever wanted to do was help people."

"A noble endeavor."

"Today it might not matter so much as medical marijuana is legal in the state, but back then it wasn't. But the stigma is real. It would be like getting caught drunk on the job. Not good."

"I understand the severity of that. As a law enforcement officer, that's a serious thing."

"It is and I complied. I never deliberately took drugs. I would never have jeopardized my job or my work."

"Then what happened?"

"Someone delivered brownies to my house—on my birthday. I had no idea they were laced with pot. Before I went to bed, I enjoyed several with a glass of milk and the next morning I had my blood test."

"Which you failed."

"And subsequently got kicked off the force. If it hadn't been for Colfax Security giving me a second chance, I don't know where I'd be today. All I ever wanted to do was protect and serve. You know?"

"So, you said, and you have...and still are."

"Not that it matters much now. Basically, I'm back where I started. Without a job, bills to pay..."

"You do realize you were set up?"

"I know."

"Tiffany?"

"Most likely, although when I confronted her, she denied it."

"Did you believe her?"

"I'm not sure it matters anymore. Tiffany was never afraid to admit to her shenanigans. She reveled in letting me know the deed had been done by her. To deny this one, would have been so unlike her. Although, I suspect Tiffany had her hand in this latest thing."

"As did Pricilla. Of that, I'm certain."

The color faded from Samantha's face. "Pricilla? Are you serious?"

He nodded. "Do you trust me?"

She locked her gaze with his. "Yes. Of course."

"Look, I know you think this is about me, and it is, but it's also now about you." He held up the ring. "And I'm in no mood to let Pricilla and Tiffany win."

When Sam got home, ready to lay into Tiffany for her despicable behavior, she found both Tiff and her stepmother in the living room packing.

"What's going on here?"

"Looks like the house is to be auctioned next week," Katherine said.

"That's impossible. We're still behind, but I've been making the payments. I'd worked everything out with the bank."

"Here's the letter from them."

Sam perused the document. "This shows three withdrawals in the past week." She eyed Tiffany. "Did you do this?"

"I'm not on the account." She rolled up a figurine in packing paper, then set it next to several other pieces.

"But you're responsible, aren't you? Memory lapses or not, Katherine wouldn't have done this unless you were behind it."

"It was supposed to be a small loan—to impress Jason. I'd planned to put the money back before the next mortgage payment came due."

"Put it back? How? You don't make any money." Anger flared in her gut. "How could you? Are you really that selfish—that hateful? You've caused me to lose my job and now you've robbed us of our home."

"You can't snag a wealthy husband unless you can play the part." She shrugged, picked up one of the wrapped objects and placed it in a box. "And I'm not sorry, because it worked. Jason has graciously asked Mom and me to stay with him a while."

"Keep your fingers crossed," Katherine said. "I think wedding bells are in our future."

Speechless, Sam focused her attention on her stepmother's proclamation, then turned toward Tiffany. "I take it I'm not included in the invitation, not that I would have accepted."

"I'm sure you'll figure something out. Why don't you ask Prince Charming for help? Oh, I know, maybe you could stay with those old people you care so much about."

She clenched her jaw. "Maybe I will."

CHAPTER 18

Marcus lightly touched Samantha's back as she strolled by his side as Mitchell Pierce, the president of the Meadowbrook Polo Club, finished up the short tour of the clubhouse. Eliza had chosen a lovely black wool dress for her and low-heeled boots appropriate for touring the grounds.

With the tour of the barns behind them, they entered the clubhouse for lunch. Walnut paneled-walls and paintings from polo matches hung throughout the building. They stopped in front of one in particular, which depicted King Maxwell on his champion horse.

Marcus folded his arms and studied the oil painting. The artist had certainly captured his father's handsome features and the intensity in his eyes that Marcus knew well.

"He looks like you," Samantha said.

"He was about my age here."

"Your father was a great friend to us," Mitchell said. "His charitable contributions went far beyond the financial, as his personal appearances here and on the polo field brought world-wide recognition to our club."

"My father loved Meadowbrook's rich history and tradition, making his involvement here an easy decision."

They continued to the dining hall where guests were already taking their assigned seats.

Samantha had been seated to his right and Mitchell to his left. Several times during the meal he caught Samantha staring at her plate or off into the distance. Except for her polite responses to the person on her right, she spoke very little during the meal and his attempts to engage her fell flat.

Something obviously had her preoccupied. He wondered if it had something to do with Blake and Colfax Security. He found himself wishing the meal and ceremony over so he could quiz her.

The unveiling of the statue followed the luncheon. The bigger than life, bronze likeness of the king moved him, more so, when a feminine hand clasped his from underneath the table. He glanced right and locked his gaze with Samantha's. Her lovely smile and the squeeze of her fingers warmed his heart.

"A proud moment for you," she said.

He nodded.

After the ceremony, Marcus and Sam said their goodbyes to Mitchell and to the rest of Meadowbrook's staff. On the drive back to the hotel he shifted in his seat to get a better view of her profile. For a moment he watched how the streetlights cast their synchronized pattern across her somber features.

"Penny for them," he asked.

She blinked and glanced his way. A small smile hovered over her mouth, then disappeared when she licked her lips.

"I'm sorry. I know I've not been the best company today." She sighed. "I received some rather bad news earlier."

"Anything you care to tell me."

"No. It's nothing to do with you. Just something I need to put my mind to sooner than I'd thought. It'll be all right."

"You're sure you don't want my help?"

"Yes, I'm sure, but thank you."

"A shoulder to cry on, then?"

She shifted toward him. "I'm not at the crying stage yet, but if and when I am, I'll keep your shoulder in mind." She smiled sweetly, locking her gaze with his.

CHAPTER 19

Sam left The Carlyle early. Once outside, she grabbed a taxi to her home. She missed being a part of Colfax Security. It had been a stabling force in her life for several years now. At least she still had her work with the prince. She had no idea what she'd do once that job came to an end.

It took every ounce of mental fortitude not to panic over her future. She told herself to enjoy the day. After all, not everyone got the chance to Christmas shop with a prince.

The sun had just come up when Sam exited the taxi. She made a beeline to her Volkswagen. She climbed in and turned on the ignition, then rubbed her hands together while the car warmed up. She wanted to get back to The Carlyle before the prince even knew she'd left.

Back in the hotel, she changed into a pair of jeans and bulky wool sweater, then joined him in his suite for breakfast.

"I was beginning to think I'd have to wake you." His warm gaze met hers from across the room.

"Sorry." She sat down as Percy filled her cup with coffee.

"You seem to be feeling better this morning."

"I am." She nodded and smiled.

"So. Have you decided where you'd like to shop today?" Marcus said.

"I have."

"And?"

"It's a surprise."

"Really."

"Yep." Sam buttered a slice of warm toast, took a bite, then settled her gaze on him. "You trust me, right?"

"The fact you're asking me that now has me worried." He lifted the corner of his mouth and leveled her with his crooked smile. That and the affectionate glint coming from his brown-eyed gaze had her pulse racing.

Her heart fluttered with the same giddy feeling she'd experienced as a young teen while staring longingly at his poster. Except he was no longer paper and ink, but flesh and blood and *real* and sitting across from her discussing their upcoming day together.

How in the world did this happen? To her—Samantha Keller—plain-Jane security officer.

For years she'd crushed on a young man she'd only read about, a prince she'd only seen on paper. Allowing her heart to feel, where he was concerned, was completely foolish and dangerous on her part.

But she couldn't help herself and counted each day with Marcus as a gift, until her time with him ended. Every day in his company had been beyond wonderful. Magical even.

When it came to the prince, it was a challenge to hold herself together. He took her breath away. And as the days went by, she found it more and more difficult to separate the dream from reality.

"No need to worry," she said. "It'll be fun. I promise."

He stood and placed his hand on the back of her chair. "Lucky for you, I like surprises. Let's go."

The doorman greeted Sam and Marcus as they passed through. Once on the street, Marcus stopped.

"So, where to?" he said.

"Your chariot awaits, Your Highness." Sam pointed with all the reverence of a royal servant toward her yellow Volkswagen.

"You're kidding."

"Nope. Today, I set the rules." She walked to the driver's side and motioned for him to get in.

"You're comfortable driving in the city?"

"Of course. I grew up here. That said, we're leaving Manhattan. I thought it would be nice to get away from the media for the day."

"You really think we can escape the paparazzi?"

"Yes, especially since I posted that you would be hosting a few friends for brunch at La Mercerie. It's forty minutes from here in Soho."

"Ah, so while the media are waiting for us to show up there, we'll be long gone in the opposite direction."

"That's right."

"So where are you taking me?"

"To Hudson, New York. It's about an hour's drive from here."

"And why choose Hudson?"

"For its charm and antique shops and most of all for the scenic drive."

"Too bad it's not warmer. It would've been fun to let down the top of your car."

"Yeah, I thought about putting it down, but it is rather chilly."

"I'll have to come back in the spring, then," he said.

She cut her eyes in his direction. Marcus sat gazing out the window with a pensive expression on his face. Sometimes he said the oddest things. His statement reminded her that the ring on her left hand was nothing more than a prop for his latest fictional play on the world's stage.

Although the hardwood trees had lost their leaves, the rolling hills and curving backroads still held the serene beauty the drive was known for.

Forty-five minutes later, they entered the outskirts of Hudson. The picturesque town oozed nineteenth century charm. Holiday lights and garland with silver and gold ornaments dressed the old-fashioned street-lamps along the drive into the town center. Sam pulled the bug into the first spot she came to on Warren Street.

"What a delightful place." The prince got out of the car and met her on the sidewalk. "Very Christmassy."

"It is. You just missed Winter Walk. Thousands come for it. The streets are lit with white lights and there're Christmas carolers, fireworks—It's quite a festival."

"Sounds like it. The nineteenth century architecture is pristine, and I can see why you wanted me to see it."

She glanced at him with some confusion.

"I assumed you knew about my interest in architecture," he said.

"You assumed right. I thought you'd especially like seeing Rivertown Lodge. Originally built as a movie theatre in the late '20s, it's now a modern twenty-seven room hotel. And the three-story Victorian homes on Willard Place are a must see."

"I look forward to it. But I'm still curious as to how you know so much about me."

She gaped at him and by the startled look on her face, he'd taken her by surprise.

"I...told you. I read about you in preparation for this assignment."

"My interest in architecture is fairly well known, but as to the charity I started with my father... Not so much." He locked his gaze with hers, daring her to disagree.

"Is that so?"

"Yes. I actually looked it up after you mentioned it the other night and found absolutely nothing."

"I know I read about it somewhere. How else could I've known about it?"

"How else, indeed?"

The question was moot as he strolled off leaving her to stand on the sidewalk. She blinked and quickly caught up with him.

As they walked along, she glanced at his profile. "There're times when I think I'd enjoy living in a small town." Which wasn't at all true, but she experienced a strong desire to push forward to another subject and felt discussing the merits of small-town living as safe as any.

"Sterlyn has many such towns and villages in our little kingdom. I'd love to show them to you sometime."

"That sounds lovely, but unrealistic."

"In what way?"

"Well, this thing we have," she fluttered her hand between them, "is not real."

"Oh, right. Of course."

"That said, I would love to visit your country. You know... Someday."

"I would like that."

Sam walked into the first shop they came to on Warren Street. The conversation had taken a turn to the uncomfortable, and she thought it best to move along.

She strolled through the boutique, feigning interest in several different items, until she spotted a pretty glass angel on the next table.

"How lovely." She picked it up and laid it across her palm. "I used to have one like this. Except it was plastic, not crystal. I'd pretend she was my protection, my guardian angel." Sam checked the price and blanched. Way too expensive for her pocketbook. She set it down, carefully.

"Don't you like it?"

"Yes, it's just a bit pricy for me."

"Are you shopping for anyone in particular?"

She nodded. "I want to get something for each of the residents at Oakland Manor. And for my Steps, of course. But I'm afraid the items in this store are way over my budget. How about you?"

"Percy usually makes most of the appropriate purchases on my behalf."

"Seriously? You don't do your own shopping?"

He smiled. "I can see I've offended your sensibilities. As Prince of Sterlyn, I'm obligated to give gifts to many people not only in Sterlyn but in other countries, as well. But when it comes to my mother and our staff, I chose those gifts myself. And if it makes you feel any better, I do have to approve whatever Percy picks out. And he is not without help on that score. There are others who assist him."

"I see."

"So. Have I redeemed myself in your critical eyes?"

She broke into a wide smile. "Yes, you have."

Sam had success in the next few stores they entered. She found several items perfect for the residents and even a gift for Katherine. Finding something for Tiffany created more of a challenge.

"Why are you struggling with what to buy your step-sister?"

"Truthfully, I don't know why. She's very particular and hard to buy for."

"Are you trying to win her approval?"

"Of course not. That's silly."

"Is it?"

She stared at him as if he could read her thoughts. She pressed her lips together and glanced around the shop. "You have this uncanny way of seeing right through me. How is that?"

"I have a knack for reading people. For instance, your instinct to protect others extends even to those who've hurt you. Because of that pain, you want to please them with the hope that they will finally accept you."

"Wow. You are good." She plopped the item on the counter and pulled out a twenty. "It's a good thing my pocketbook is lacking. Otherwise, just think of the money I'd be spending on Tiffany right now."

She thanked the clerk, then left the store.

Once outside, Marcus grabbed her arm. "Hey. I didn't mean to hurt your feelings."

"You didn't." She sighed and raised her gaze to his. "And you're right. I've been trying to win her affection for years. And now, thanks to you, I hate myself for it."

He released her arm but didn't move away, sending her an open invitation to confide in him. His mere presence comforted her. All masculine and totally wonderful.

What was happening to her? None of this was real, yet she found it impossible to resist the warmth and intensity of his gaze.

Spellbound. That's what she was. He'd cast his royal, handsome, princely spell on her. His presence utterly and completely overwhelmed. She swallowed.

"After my dad and Katherine married, I was beyond thrilled at having an older sister. I'd always wanted a sibling and I finally had one. But over time, their presence in our home became a daily trial for me, more so after my dad died. I'd longed for Katherine to comfort me, for a sister's hug. But I didn't get any. Not then—not now."

"I'm sorry. And sorry I brought the subject up."

"I stopped having a pity-party a long time ago." She swiped at an angry tear. "And I'm certainly not going to wallow in one now."

"You're crying?"

"Oh really? What gave me away?"

"And you resort to sarcasm and to putting up walls to protect yourself." He placed his hands on her shoulders. "If I may make one more observation."

"Only one?"

He gave her a sympathetic smile. "You're a proud woman and you feel it's somehow weak on your part to share your burdens with others."

She crossed her arms and glared at him.

"I know there's something more. You've been preoccupied since our dinner at the polo club. You can talk to me."

She could feel herself weakening.

"So, what do you say, over lunch?"

She signed and nodded.

CHAPTER 20

They stopped at Grazin' Diner for lunch.

After they ordered burgers and fries, Marcus reached across the table and took hold of Samantha's hand. She stared, wordlessly.

Thankful when she hadn't withdrawn it, he gently fingered her engagement ring.

"It looks good on you."

"It's beautiful and terrifying."

"I get the beautiful part, but—"

"I'm afraid I'll lose it."

He squeezed her hand. "You won't. And if you do, it's insured."

"That doesn't make me feel any better."

He released her hand and sat back as the waitress placed their meals in front of them.

He dipped a fry in catsup. "So. I'm all ears."

She chomped down on a French fry, then swigged her Coke. "You are one persistent prince."

He rested his forearms on the table. "I know there's more to that one lone tear. So out with it." He held her gaze until she finally relented.

"About six months ago my stepmother took out a second mortgage on our house and didn't tell me until recently. I'd worked out a payment schedule with the bank, then yesterday I found out Tiffany has been withdrawing money, leaving very little for the payments."

"How long has this been going on?"

"Months."

"Do you need financial help? I'm happy to—"

"No. Please no. This is why I didn't want to tell you. The money's not the problem." She lowered her gaze and bit into a pickle slice. "I just need to pay better attention."

"Sounds like you need to take full control of the finances."

"I thought I had. I chose to have Katherine on the account in case something happened to me. But that was before she…"

"Started to forget?"

She nodded. "I've now set up a separate account and will deposit my checks in that one. My Steps are not on it." She lifted the top bun and tipped the white onion slice off the burger with her fork.

A stubborn expression covered her face, signaling the subject was now closed. But something told him the new account wouldn't be enough and that her efforts were most likely too little-too late.

"Are you certain there's nothing I can do to assist you?"

"I'm sure." Her lips tilted into a half-smile. "But, thank you."

There it was again—that wall of self-preservation. He sensed there was more to her distress but chose not to press her on it. Samantha had a habit of tugging on his heart strings. It pained him to see her unhappy. He had this sudden urge to protect her, not just now, but always.

"Enough about me," she said, breaking into his thoughts. "Tell me more about your interest in architecture?"

"I attribute my love for the subject from my father. He studied architecture at university."

"I would have thought a future king would study things like foreign policy and politics."

"Not necessarily. I've been groomed and prepared for the duties of the office long before university. Of course, one may supplement his or her education on foreign policy while at school, but the years of instruction on such matters are already ingrained in us from childhood."

"Doesn't sound like you have much choice in the matter."

"Well, technically I do. But I wouldn't, of course. Even if I had a sibling to take the reins, I would never abdicate the throne or the responsibilities that go with it. To fail to fulfill my duty would be irresponsible. To cripple the monarchy would be unconscionable."

"Spoken like Sterlyn's future king. And since we're speaking our minds, why not apply those same principles to your dealings with your mother and Pricilla?"

"My fencing coach would appreciate your straight-on attack, for both its thrust and precision."

She grinned. "Oh, to please someone in your kingdom is high praise indeed. Especially for a lowly girl from Queens."

Her eyes held an impish twinkle he found hard to resist. And that wasn't the only thing. He'd succumbed to her forthright attitude, her selfless nature, and to her engaging smile. And her recent vulnerability touched him immensely. He knew it had taken a lot for her to trust him.

"Have I told you how great you look today."

"I'm wearing jeans and a sweater."

"I know but that shade of yellow brings out the highlights in your hair—the blue in your eyes. One of ours?"

"You know it is."

He grinned. "You don't take compliments very well, either. We'll have to work on that."

* * *

As they stood to leave, Sam heard the faint buzz of a cell phone.

"That's me," Marcus said, as he pulled it from his jacket. "I need to take this. It'll only take a few minutes."

"That's fine. I need to look for a few more gifts. Meet me at Harvey's Counter. It's a block or so down from here."

At Harvey's, Sam found a wonderful coffee table book of Hudson's historic Victorian houses for Marcus. She'd wanted to get him a Christmas gift, and this one seemed perfect. The photographs of the homes were fabulous. If nothing else, it would be a nice keepsake for him when he returned to Sterlyn.

The store attendant had just placed the wrapped book in a shopping bag when Marcus pushed through Harvey's entrance. He carried a small bag in his left hand.

"Seems you've done a bit of shopping yourself."

He glanced at his package, then back at her. "Proof that I actually do buy the occasional gift."

"So. Is everything okay?"

He tilted his head sideways.

"Your call."

"Uh, yes. At least I hope so."

"That doesn't sound good."

"It's a business thing. I do need to head back to sign some papers, though. So, if you're done with your shopping, shall we go?"

"Of course."

On the drive back to the city Sam wondered what this business thing could be and what had been so important that they had to cut short their shopping day.

CHAPTER 21

Sam, Marcus, and Percy sat at the round table in the presidential suite scrutinizing the guest list for the Christmas Eve Gala. The past several days had flown by with three more parties, two luncheons and a ribbon cutting in the city.

As much as Sam hated to admit it, the gala signaled the end of Marcus' visit. She would miss him terribly when he returned to Sterlyn and cherished every moment they'd spent together. Her life would never be the same for having known him. She loved him—not with some girlhood crush—but with the *until death do us part* kind of love. There were moments when she thought he might feel the same. She'd hold onto those until they said goodbye.

She ran her gaze down the page to the D's and then the O's. No Draper or Osbourne was on the list. Even so, she knew Tiffany would find a way to be in attendance. She checked the R's. Pricilla's name spread across the sheet in bold black ink.

"Are you looking for anyone in particular," Percy said.

"No. Just giving it a last-minute review. You're certain this is the final list?" she said.

"Yes, but it's common at functions such as this to have some eleventh-hour changes. Our security detail is fully capable of handling them." Percy stood. "If that's all, I have a meeting with the caterer."

Marcus reached across the table and took Sam's hand. "I know you're worried about Pricilla being on the guest list. She's in New York and it would be extremely odd for her not to be in attendance. But remember, you're coming as my betrothed. There's nothing she can do to change that."

"That may be true, but you don't know Tiffany."

* * *

That afternoon, Sam stopped by the house to check her mail. Neither Tiffany nor Katherine were there. She found a small stack of envelopes and magazines on the parlor room desk. She flipped through, tossing the junk. Her hand stilled as her gaze fell on the next letter. It'd come from Community Bank. *This can't be good.* Heart pounding, she ripped open the envelope.

Eviction Notice splayed in bold print across the top of the letter. She swallowed, licked her lips and stared at the sheet of paper. Her hands trembled as she refolded the letter and stuffed it back into the envelope.

By the time she'd arrived at the bank, her stomach had twisted in knots. Five minutes later she sat across from Mr. Meyers.

"I just need another extension, time to build up my new checking account, if—"

"Samantha. The note has been paid off. The house is no longer yours," he said. "The eviction letter had been sent."

"Someone bought my house?" To her dismay, her voice broke.

"I'm sorry."

She had no idea how long she sat there staring at him. Her mind searched for something else to say, but she couldn't think of another thing. Mr. Meyers cleared his throat and shoveled papers across his desk.

She took that as her cue to say something or leave. "My personal things are still in there. I haven't had a chance to clear them out."

"The personal items still belong to you. The buyer won't be taking over the house until after the new year. Does that give you enough time to put your things in order?"

She sniffed and nodded.

As she stood to leave, she asked, "Who's the buyer?"

"I believe it's an architectural firm." He shuffled through the papers. "I'll have to look up the name—"

"Don't bother. It doesn't really matter at this point."

Back home, she entered the house through the front door. Disappointment swelled in her chest and squeezed her heart. Swiping at a tear, she sat down and gazed around the parlor in confusion. "How did this happen?" She placed both hands over her aching heart.

Choking back tears, she stood and headed for the stairs.

She flipped the light switch as she entered her room. The poster of the prince still hung on the wall. Except for the photos of her and her dad, there wasn't much she wanted. She took off the poster, rolled it up, and set it in the corner.

She checked her stepsister's room. All of her personal things had been cleared out. Just as well. Tiffany was the last person she wanted to see right now. A quick check in Katherine's, and it looked like most of her belongings were gone, as well. Sam checked the chest of drawers. They were empty.

The next few hours passed in a daze. She meandered through the rest of the house like a zombie. She needed a plan. She'd have to take inventory. The sooner the better.

None of the furniture had been moved yet. She wondered if Katherine or Tiffany would like to have any of the pieces. At some point she'd have to make a list of what to keep and what to let go.

By the time she'd left the house, she'd come up with a simple plan to get her through the new year when the architectural firm took over. She'd stay at the hotel for the remainder of the prince's visit and then see if she could stay at the manor for a few days. At least that would give her a week or so to find a new place.

A quick call to Caroline secured her stay for as long as they had the house.

"Are you kidding? You're one of the few people who really care about them," Caroline said. "They'll love having you here."

Sam went through the rest of the day making a list and organizing some of her things. She had another party to attend that evening, and it was imperative she get her act together. The prince could not know about this latest event. She would not have his pity. It would be far too humiliating.

Sam pasted on a smile and entered the royal suite. Eliza already had her dress and heels laid out for the evening at the Plaza Hotel.

"Wow, this dress is gorgeous," she said, in an effort to stay upbeat. "Let me guess, the prince's selection?"

"No. Mine." Eliza beamed.

"Nice job."

After Sam showered, she sat at the dressing table and applied her makeup, then turned to Eliza for approval. "What do you think?"

"A touch more eye shadow should do it." She tilted her head and ran her gaze over Sam's face. "And a bit more pink on your lips."

"Eliza, I can't tell you enough how much your help has meant to me these past two weeks. I couldn't have done any of this without you."

"Thank you, miss. It's been my pleasure to assist you."

Eliza helped Sam slip on the dress and, after one last look in the mirror, she joined the prince.

"Wow, you look amazing," Marcus said, taking her hands in his. "Tonight's assembly will be most jealous of you." The warmth of his smile echoed in his voice and sent her pulses racing.

"Let's just hope Pricilla is among the jealous. She's the only one I'm worried about. Has she called it off with you yet? You'd tell me if she had, right? We only have a few more days until you leave. And I'm afraid your plan may not be working."

"Hey, stop for a breath." A delicious deep laugh

rom within him. "Let me worry about Pri-
.." He gave her hands a gentle shake. "You just continue to be your wonderful self. And gaze at me
adoringly when we dance."

The latter would not be hard at all. Not one little bit.

The antique clock on the wall chimed midnight, signaling the end to the evening's festivities. Sam had
happily played her part well, adoring gaze and all.

After selecting a fizzy drink from the bar, she stood
next to a Queen Anne chair sipping the sweet liquid.
Across the room, Marcus engaged an older couple in
conversation.

She loved these moments, when she could watch
him without his being aware. It reminded her of how
she used to stare with longing at his poster. She
clamped her lower lip with her teeth. Gazing at the
real man was far more wonderful. Dressed in a navy
suit that fit him to perfection, he was, hands down, the
best-looking man in the room.

She took a sip of her drink and strolled the outer
edges of the dance floor. Escort or not, she'd made it a
practice of searching the faces of the guests at all the
events the prince attended. It may not have been what
she'd been hired for, but her DNA decreed she protect
and serve. It just didn't feel right not to.

As she rounded the back corner of the room, sh
caught a familiar voice coming from the other side of
the column to her left.

"I have to say, I've sold my stepsister short over the
years." Tiffany spoke in a begrudging tone.

Tiffany. Of course, she'd be lurking around here
somewhere. Sam had no doubt her Step's late arrival
was due to Pricilla's scheming.

Sam had never been one to gloat but embraced a
slight rush of pleasure at her stepsister's admittance.
She stayed hidden behind the column, interested in
hearing more.

"For her to attract Prince Marcus is quite remarkable," Tiffany added.

"Nothing remarkable about it," Pricilla said. "The
queen selected Samantha's photo from a stack of Colfax
security's female officers, because of her unattractive
appearance. And believe me, he was most unhappy
with his mother's choice. But I agree, the change in her
is amazing and most likely due to the challenge."

"What challenge?"

"That he would never be able to turn her into
princess material. To which he responded, 'give me a
month and I will.'"

"I heard he extended his stay until after Christmas.
Do you think that's the reason?" Tiffany laughed.

Sam stood frozen, unable to move or to think. Blood pounded in her temples. Her breath quickened. Her cheeks became warm. She felt a nauseating sinking of despair. Blinking back tears, she skirted the column, and hugged the back wall as she made her way to the exit.

CHAPTER 22

Sharp, cold bit Sam in the face as she exited the Plaza, with misery so acute that it was a physical pain. How could she have been such a fool? To have trusted him, poured her heart out to him, while he used her in some bet with Pricilla, no less.

This whole time she'd thought he'd changed. That he'd returned to his former wonderful self. The prince of her childhood. But he hadn't. He was calculating and self-centered. Conceited and spoiled. Expecting the world to revolve around him and his wishes.

As much as she tried to hold back the tears, they still came. Waves of sorrow turned to chest-racking sobs. She claimed the nearest bench, threw her arms around her torso and cried.

It wasn't long before the cold seeped to her bones. She sniffed and lifted her head. "Miss Ellie?" Sam looked right, then left. "How in the—What in the world are you doing here?"

"I took a taxi." Miss Ellie smiled endearingly.

"At this time of night?"

"You forget. This is my old stomping ground."

"Of course. Broadway. But should you be alone, I mean—"

"Look at you. Your face is a mess..." She shook her head. "Back into the hotel with you. This is no way to leave a party."

"You don't understand. I can't go back."

Miss Ellie placed her hands on each side of Sam's face. "You can because you're a strong cup of tea."

Miss Ellie was right. Sam had never run from her problems. And she wasn't about to start now. She blew into her hands and followed Miss Ellie to the main entrance.

"Now go freshen up," she said. "I'll see you later."

At that moment, a taxi pulled up. Sam helped the little lady into the back seat, then waved as the taxi pulled away from the curb.

Once inside, she stopped in the first ladies' room she came to. After freshening up, she stared at her reflection in the mirror. She would finish the ruse with Marcus, help rid him of Pricilla, then quit.

Now, how best to rid him of Pricilla—once and for all.

Ten minutes later, she entered the ballroom. Head held high, she pasted on a smile and scanned the ornate hall. Fighting back her earlier humiliation, she stood off-stage gathering strength for the performance of a lifetime. Thinking of Miss Ellie, Sam was reminded of her words that day at the manor.

'You are the author of your life... It's you who writes your own story. How you think of yourself is who you are.'

Sam spotted the prince dancing with Pricilla. She knew exactly what she had to do. It was now or never. Drawing strength from her hurt and anger, she walked with all the poise and authority she could muster across the dance floor. When she reached the couple, she tapped Pricilla on the shoulder.

"Excuse me, but may I cut in?" She flicked a sparkling smile to Marcus and then to Pricilla. The look in Pricilla's eyes was priceless. Astounded didn't even come close. Horrified may have been a better word.

Sam watched as her expression turned to spitting anger. If the woman before her said no, then Sam had no idea what she'd do next. So, she stood her ground, hoping protocol would win the day.

Pricilla leveled Sam a vile look that said she may have won this round, but not so the next. "Of course," Pricilla said, all proper and in control.

Marcus took Sam in his arms, momentarily speechless in his surprise. "Well done, Samantha."

Done, being the operative word, Your Highness and what you and I will be soon.

"I've been looking for you for twenty minutes. But I have to say, I'm surprised, if not elated, at your nerve. Never in my wildest dreams would I have thought to witness such...an audacious spirit from you." He eyed her with an appreciative gleam.

"Hardly what one would expect from an unattractive person as myself, right?"

"I thought you were over such beliefs."

She raised her arms and laced them around his neck, pulling him closer. "Oh, I am. And the one thing I'm thankful for after having spent time in your company."

"Only one?" He gazed searchingly into her eyes. "I'd hoped—"

She placed a finger to his lips. "Shut up and dance, Your Highness. We still have many guests to deceive."

She lay her head on his shoulder. More to avoid his searching gaze than for anything else.

* * *

Marcus continued to hold her close. As delightful as it was to have her pressed sweetly against him, he knew something wasn't right. The fact that she'd disappeared, then returned masquerading as a completely different person was reason to be alarmed.

As he held her, he scanned the dance floor and spotted Pricilla and Tiffany leaving the ballroom. Tiffany had not been invited and yet she was here. Pricilla probably bribed someone to get her access to the party. He'd never known her not to get anything she'd set her mind to.

He glanced at the top of Samantha's head. A sweet scent of lilacs wafted from her hair. She pressed against him, all feminine, all woman. He'd daydreamed about such a moment. Holding her like this, as if she belonged to him. Having her in his arms was absolute heaven.

When the dance ended, he walked Samantha to the wine bar. "Would you like a drink?"

"I'd love one."

"She'll have a sparkling wi—"

"Bourbon on the rocks," she said.

His head swiveled toward her. "I'll...have the same." Surprised by her choice of drink would be an understatement. "I never took you for a bourbon woman."

"Then you don't know me."

"On the contrary—"

She raised her chin and shot him a cold stare.

"I...stand corrected." He gazed at her as if his continued perusal would shed light on the matter. "Have I done something to offend you?"

"Not in the least." She patted his arm, then smiled and waved at someone across the room.

"I beg to differ." He took hold of her wrist and led her to a quiet corner. He sat down, pulling her with him, giving her no choice but to sit.

She took a sip of her drink, refusing to look at him.

He laid his arm on the back of the love seat. "Samantha. What is it? What happened?"

She continued to stare at nothing in particular in front of her.

"Was it Pricilla? Did she say anything to you to upset you?"

She turned to him. "What could she have possibly said to upset me?"

Actually, he could think of several things. More than he cared to admit.

She quirked a brow and, God help him, stared at him in a haughty manner so like Pricilla that he almost burst out laughing. Except nothing about this was funny.

The scathing look Samantha gave him mirrored one he'd seen many times by the upper echelon of society. Had he done this to her, with all of his lessons and tutorials?

"I hope my little performance has put Pricilla off, once and for all. But if it hasn't, I still have one more surprise up my sleeve." She stood and pinned him with a bland expression. "If you'll excuse me, Your Highness. I must powder my nose."

She strolled off with all the elegance of a princess, except the inner princess qualities he'd come to admire in her seemed to have suddenly disappeared.

CHAPTER 23

This was it. Christmas Eve. The final act. The night of the gala. She'd spent the day going through the things at her home, crying on and off throughout the day as she wrapped up china and crystal and other personal items that had belonged to her mother. She wasn't sure if her tears were for the loss of her home or from discovering how Marcus had used her. Both events had broken her heart.

How could he have done this to her? She'd deliberately stayed away from the hotel so she wouldn't have to see him. She'd mulled over their time together. He'd been a royal pain at first, but as the days went by, what they'd shared seemed real and genuine—honest and intimate.

She rested her head in her hands. No use in trying to figure it out. She glanced at the wall clock, wondering how she would get through this evening. It was getting late, and Eliza would be in a tizzy wondering where she was.

Sam stared at her reflection in the full-length mirror. Eliza had chosen an exquisite Oscar de la Renta for her to wear this evening.

"Time to go, miss. Prince Marcus will be so pleased when he sees you."

"Thank you." Poor Eliza. She'd been clueless from the start, and Sam felt it better to keep it that way. She hated deceiving her.

Carrying a small, beaded clutch, she walked down the wide hallway that led to the ballroom. As she rounded the corner, Pricilla jumped out from behind a massive ornate column dressed in a shimmering blue evening gown.

Sam jumped and stopped mid-stride.

Eyes dark and accusing, Pricilla planted herself in front of Sam like an avenging angel—sword raised, ready for battle. Except her weapon was a long-stemmed glass of red wine.

Before Sam could get a word out, Pricilla raised her glass and threw the blood-red liquid on Sam's dress.

Sam sucked in a sharp breath and stood gasping in shock. Shock turned to distress, distress to anger.

"Are you crazy?"

"You will never have him." Pricilla spat the words. In that moment her snarl erased every bit of her natural beauty.

Sam stood, shaking and stunned, as Pricilla stormed off. She fingered the bodice of the dress, a million thoughts running through her head. She glanced ahead and behind her, wondering if anyone had seen the attack. Not sure what to do, she ran back to her suite.

"Eliza!" She screeched, but she'd already gone. Sam pulled on her overcoat, snatched up her clutch and left.

She sat in the back seat of the taxi and wiped her tears. The multi-colored chorus of lights scrolled by her window mocking her with their joyful, glittering refrain. This was not at all how she'd imagined Christmas Eve would go. Just as well. She was tired of the deception. Her stomach churned as she thought of how the news media would spin her departure from the gala.

The house was in darkness when she arrived. As the taxi drove off, she checked her clutch for the key. It wasn't there. Her heart sank. She must have left it back at the hotel.

She gazed down the street and watched the taxi's taillights disappear at the next corner. If only she'd had the forethought to have the driver wait. At least the manor was only a short walk away. It was early, which meant there'd be plenty of people still on the streets.

It was well after eight when she arrived. She tiptoed through the foyer careful not to disturb any of the residents watching TV. Plus, she was way too upset to face anyone at the moment.

She mounted the stairway, lifted her long skirt and dashed up the steps to find the hallway empty. Good. She'd not be waylaid here either. She stepped through the door of the temporary bedroom Caroline Hill had given her. She hugged her torso and wrapped herself in a cocoon of anguish, then sat on her bed. Tears slowly found their way down her cheeks until deep sobs racked her insides.

"What's wrong, dear?"

Sam's head snapped up. "Miss Ellie." She hiccupped. "You scared me."

Ellie stood, hands clasped in front of her, in Sam's bedroom doorway. "I'm so sorry. I heard you crying."

"I didn't hear you come in." In her distraught state Sam wondered how she could have missed seeing her in the hallway. Sam swiped at her tears and tried to compose herself.

Miss Ellie approached. "What happened to your dress?"

"I had an accident."

"No matter. I have just the evening gown for you."

"Thanks, but I'm not going back."

"But what about the prince and your promise to him?"

"How do you know—"

"He and I had a little chat the other day."

"He came here. When?"

Miss Ellie smiled. "That story is for another day. Now come with me."

Sam, who wanted to do anything but, dutifully followed. Minutes later she stood in front of a wardrobe in Miss Ellie's apartment. Ellie opened the door, then stepped away with a flourish.

Inside hung the most beautiful green dress Sam had ever seen. It was covered in sparkly sequins and tiny stones that looked like diamonds.

Sam reverently placed her fingers along the bodice. "It feels like satin."

"It's taffeta. My favorite. Especially for Christmas."

"Miss Ellie, it's truly beautiful."

"It's yours."

"What?"

"You heard me. Now put it on. You're going back to that ball."

"It's almost nine o'clock."

"Which means it's just getting started."

* * *

Marcus kept glancing at the entrance for a sign of Samantha. Although she'd been acting strange since last night's party, he'd fully expected her to join him after Ellie did her hair, but that was more than an hour ago. And every time he headed for the door, someone grabbed his attention. He finally sent Percy to see what could be keeping her. He'd planned an extraordinary evening and if she didn't show up soon, it wouldn't be.

Percy approached him with a shake of his head.

"She's not in either suite, Your Majesty."

"Thank you, Percy." Marcus' concern grew over the next few minutes. Within the past twenty-four hours something had happened to upset Samantha. Before this night was over, he would find out what that something was.

The unexpected announcement from the royal guard had him and the rest of those in attendance stand at attention. "Queen Beatrice de Blecourt of Sterlyn."

Applause broke from the ballroom as Marcus' mother stepped through the entrance. Her smile seemed to encompass everyone present. Still considered a beautiful woman by many, the prince marveled at her grace and poise and knew his father would have been so proud of her.

He stood at the end of the red carpet and offered the traditional greeting with a kiss to her hand.

"Good evening, Mother. It's wonderful to see you, but I'd scheduled your arrival for tomorrow." He escorted her across the room to a seating area then released her hand with a slight bow.

"You know how I dislike being told what to do. Now, where is she?" Beatrice asked.

"She's not here."

Several New York dignitaries approached them.

"It seems your surprise entrance has caused a stir. So, I will leave you to mingle with New York's finest."

"Thank you. I've got it from here."

As the evening progressed, he'd lost all hope for an appearance by Samantha. His gut told him both Pricilla and Tiffany had something to do with the change in her.

He spotted his mother making her way to a small alcove. Most likely for some well-needed privacy. He crossed the room to join her and, when he neared the entrance to the alcove, Pricilla approached him.

"Hello Marcus." Pricilla glanced around the space. "Your fiancée seems to be missing."

"And just what would you know about that?"

"I heard she had an...accident with the royal gown. Wine, I think it was? Red wine." She smirked. "Such a shame, too. And on that gorgeous ivory dress. I understand it was completely ruined."

Anger swelled in his chest. "If you think for one moment your actions can deter Samantha Keller, then you are profoundly mistaken."

"The queen is fully behind my actions to bring you to your senses. As she has often said—"

The queen stepped out from the small vestibule. "Pray tell me what it is that I'm supposed to have said?"

Pricilla's jaw dropped and something close to panic covered her beautiful face.

"Your Majesty." Pricilla curtseyed. "I did not realize...I mean...that you..."

"Were listening?" The queen's features grew stern with disapproval. "After that hateful tirade, I believe you've now lost any sway you may have had with me in the past. If it wasn't for my fondness and long-time friendship with your mother, I would have you banished from Sterlyn."

Pricilla blanched and curtseyed. "I beg your pardon, ma'am."

"Now I suggest you leave before I change my mind."

As Pricilla turned to leave, Marcus grabbed her arm. "Pricilla. I'm sorry it had to end this way. I did warn you. I hope in time you'll find true love, as I have."

"Save your breath." She yanked her arm from his grasp and strode from the room.

Marcus returned to his mother's side. "Could you really have banished her?"

"Of course not." An impish grin lit her features. "I've just always wanted to say that."

He'd not seen this lighter side of his mother in many years. He raised a brow and leveled her a questioning glance.

She laid her hand on his forearm. "I feel like an old fool for having allowed myself to be manipulated by Pricilla. I had no idea she was such a spiteful woman. Please forgive me?"

"Of course, Mother."

"I also realize my desire for perfection blinded me to what's really important in life. There's no reason the royal rules and true happiness should be in competition. Rather, they should complement each other."

"Does that mean I can be crowned king without a wife at my side?"

"Sadly, no."

"I see."

"I crossed the ocean to meet my future daughter-in-law. I'm growing impatient. Now, where is she?"

"Miss Samantha Keller of Queens, New York." The royal guard announced from the ballroom entrance.

Marcus spun toward the entrance. Samantha stood with regal grace as the royal guard announced her arrival to those present. Dressed in a sparkly, Christmas green, taffeta ball gown...she was stunning.

The prince stood mesmerized as she walked toward him on the red carpet. Her golden hair had been swept up in soft curls—the perfect complement to her bare-shouldered gown. Samantha Keller was everything he'd ever dreamed about and more.

"Right there, Mother." Joy surged in his chest. "She's right there."

* * *

Sam was shocked to see the queen at the ball. Why hadn't she been told? Thankful for Eliza's recent instruction on the art of the curtsey, Sam continued to walk forward.

When she reached Marcus and the queen, she performed a shallow curtsey. "Your Majesty, it is an honor to meet you."

Queen Beatrice extended her hand. Sam glanced at Marcus. He gave a slight nod, signaling she was to accept his mother's hand.

"The honor is all mine," Beatrice said.

"Mother, may I present to you, Samantha Keller, my fiancée."

Sam's eyes briefly widened. She opened her mouth then clamped it shut. Marcus took her hand in his and led her to the dance floor as the small orchestra struck up a waltz.

"Marcus, what are you doing introducing me as your fiancée?" Her tone was sharp. "It's one thing to deceive New Yorkers and Pricilla, but your mother?"

"Did you really think the news of us would be confined to this city alone?"

"I...yes. Did you know it wouldn't?"

His lips curved into a smile. "There's so much I wanted to tell you earlier, but you were waylaid. But I promise I'll explain everything later. But first things first. Are you all right? I heard about what happened with the dress."

"I'm sure you did." She bristled.

"Pricilla has already been dealt with." He ran an appreciative glance over her. "You look amazing...and that dress...it's stunning. It's as if it were especially made for you."

"Thank you." It was all Sam could do to keep her cool. She wanted to lash out—give him a piece of her mind.

"I can't tell you how happy I am you decided to join me tonight. I figured after what Pricilla did to you... I was about to give up hope. But enough of her."

"Why didn't you tell me your mother would be here?"

"I'd hoped to surprise you."

"To further humiliate me?"

220 · DARCY FLYNN

His brow creased in concern. "Humiliate? We've spent over two weeks together. Have I done anything to deliberately embarrass you?"

Her gaze dropped from his piercing one. "Maybe not on the surface."

"You think I've done something unseemly behind your back?"

She raised her gaze to his. "Haven't you?"

He shook his head, clearly at a loss.

"You're telling me you've never discussed me with Pricilla?"

"I knew it. I knew Pricilla was behind this change in you. What did she tell you?"

The dance ended and they stood staring at each other.

"I'll spare you the details." She marched off the dance floor and headed for the exit. He caught up with her at the entrance and grabbed her arm.

"So, you're choosing to believe her over me?"

She twisted her arm and freed herself from his grasp. "I refuse to be in the company of a spoiled, self-ish man who thinks only of his own future, who's discarded everything of worth and value, and his responsibility to those less fortunate. One who uses... who uses..."

She swiped at an angry tear and raised her chin.

"And let me congratulate you on winning. Seems you've turned me into princess material in *less* than a month." With that, she picked up her skirt and ran for the elevator.

CHAPTER 24

Marcus and his mother entered his suite as Samantha prepared to leave. For a moment their gazes locked and held. It was obvious she had not expected him or his mother to follow her to the penthouse.

"Samantha, I—"

"Your Majesty," Sam said. "I'm sorry you had to come all this way to meet me. But, you see, this thing between your son and me is purely make believe. A ruse to get you and Pricilla off his back."

Marcus folded his arms and chewed the inside of his lip. He glanced at his mother who seemed not at all perturbed at the news, but on the contrary, entertained by the situation.

"But having spent time with both of them over the past couple of weeks, I can say with utmost authority that they are perfect for each other."

She pulled off the engagement ring and handed it to Marcus. "I'm sorry to have deceived you, ma'am. I'm afraid you've come all this way for nothing. If you'll excuse me."

She stormed out, leaving them both to stand staring after her.

* * *

Marcus dropped into the nearest chair and pressed his fingers to his forehead.

"My. What a remarkable young woman," Queen Beatrice said. "No one has ever spoken to me like that."

"Welcome to the club." The prince raised his gaze to find his mother's filled with merriment.

"At least now I understand why you didn't bring her to Sterlyn. Your engagement being a *ruse* and all."

"I'd planned to make my affection known to her. Confess all. But the timing and her current, personal problems made it impossible for me to do so. I mistakenly thought I could have everything worked out before you arrived."

"She is indeed a prize. What kind of a future monarch would let someone of her caliber walk out of here?"

"Are you serious? You want me to run after her?"

"Even though you're now rid of Pricilla, it seems to me you're still letting her stand in your way of happiness."

"That may be true, but as you've just witnessed, a stubborn Miss Keller has something to say about it, as well."

A thoughtful expression crossed the queen's features. "I can see my years of telling you what to do should have ended a long time ago."

"All right. Who are you and what have you done with my mother?"

She sat down next to him. "Mother being the operative word." She placed her hand on his. "Your father and I have made our share of mistakes. Our agreement with the Rothschilds having been one of them. After he died, I found a strange security in knowing you would be well established with one of the most prominent families in Sterlyn."

"I'm sorry. I don't understand. I had the security of the crown and all of Sterlyn... Of you."

"I know. But I won't always be here. Your father believed in arranged marriages. That said, I felt it important to honor his belief and his selection of Pricilla as your future bride."

"And now?"

"I don't feel that way at all." She squeezed his hand. "I cannot tell you how happy I was to hear you'd found true love. Not everyone is so fortunate."

"Thank you." He squeezed her hands, kissed her cheek and stood. "It seems I have a fake fiancée to go after."

* * *

Sam parked her Volkswagen at the side yard and climbed out, careful not to damage Miss Ellie's dress. The lights were on throughout the house.

"Katherine? Tiffany?" she yelled.

Tiffany popped from around the kitchen doorway. "It's just me. Mom's at Jason's getting ready for Christmas."

"Speaking of Christmas, your gifts are in my room. Don't leave without them."

Tiff nodded. "I'm surprised to see you here. Aren't you supposed to be at some fancy Christmas Eve ball?" She ran her gaze over Sam. "Wow, that's some dress."

"It's Miss Ellie's."

"Who?"

"She lives at the manor. Speaking of dresses. Did you know?"

Tiffany had the decency to look ashamed.

"I did. Look, I pretty much can't stand you, but even I drew the line at defacing an Oscar de la Renta."

"Wait. How did you know the dress was an Oscar de la Renta?" Sam said.

"Apparently, Queen Beatrice had it especially designed for Marcus' future bride to wear at her engagement party. And since that person was none other than Lady Pricilla—"

"Then it would've been hers to wear."

Tiffany nodded.

"No wonder she was so angry," Sam said.

"Anyway, I told Pricilla she was on her own. I was done with the whole, getting back at the prince, thing."

Sam gave a brief nod. "I'm going upstairs to change. Don't forget to come up before you head out."

When Sam entered her room, she set her suitcase aside, then plopped down on the edge of her bed. And for the second time this week, she lowered her head into her hands and cried.

Completely spent, she blew her nose, slipped out of Miss Ellie's dress, then changed into jeans and a sweater. Time to get back into reality.

After brushing her hair into a topknot, she padded to the bathroom to touch up her makeup.

Once that was done, she stared at her reflection. Hair twisted into a bun, she had reverted back to her old self, except for the makeup. She liked wearing it. Liked seeing how the right application defined and brought out her best features. *Thank you, Eliza.*

"Hey, I'm leaving." Tiffany hovered just inside the bedroom door.

"Oh, I've got your gifts." She snapped up the shopping bag from her day in Hudson. "Here you go. Just a little something for you and Katherine to open."

"Thanks. Um... I'm afraid yours got lost on the train."

Sam smiled and nodded. "No worries."

Tiffany turned to leave, stopped, then turned back. "Listen. There's something I need to tell you." She ran a finger along the rim of the shopping bag. "It's about the brownies."

Sam stiffened and held herself perfectly still.

"It was supposed to be a joke. A stupid prank. You were always so disgustingly perfect."

"Perfect?"

"You know. Always obeying the rules, doing the right thing, going the extra mile. I wanted to see you lose control for a change—act silly."

"I always suspected you were behind it."

"There's more."

A lump caught in Sam's throat.

"I ... I didn't know about the upcoming drug test, but..."

"But, what?"

"Mom did."

Sam swallowed hard. "Katherine?"

"She knew what I'd planned, and she didn't stop

me. I swear I didn't know. I never meant for you to lose your job." Tiffany dropped her gaze.

"I see."

"She doesn't remember having had a part in it. I hope you can forgive her, and me, too, for that matter. Believe it or not she's grown more and more fond of you as her memory fails."

Sam gave a slight nod and stuffed her hands into her pockets. "Thanks for telling me."

Sam should be angry, but she wasn't. Besides she had her immediate future to worry about and a broken heart to heal.

"You know, Jason has plenty of room, if you can't find a place to stay—"

"I'm fine, thanks," Sam said.

Tiffany nodded and left.

For a second, Sam stared at Tiff's departing figure. She'd assumed seeing her after everything that had happened would've been weird, but it hadn't been so bad. And learning the truth about the brownies had, at least, brought some closure.

The relief and contrite look in Tiffany's eyes had moved her. There had definitely been a change in her stepsister. Maybe Jason was the one for her after all.

Hands on hips, she surveyed her stuff and decided to grab a couple of boxes from the second-floor attic.

Keep busy, Sam. That's the key to getting over heartache.

CHAPTER 25

Marcus told Raymond, his limo driver, to wait for him and got out. The glowing lights from inside Samantha's house were a good sign she was there. A few seconds later, he stood at the front door and knocked. He'd played over and over in his mind what he wanted to say when he saw her. The door opened.

"Good evening, Tiffany."

"Good evening yourself." Her left eyebrow rose a fraction and she smiled.

"Is Saman—"

"She's upstairs. First room on the left." She stepped right to go around him.

"Are you leaving?"

"Yes, Mother and Jason are waiting." She stopped and glanced toward the top of the stairs, then back at him. "Good luck."

"Happy Christmas," he said.

"You, too."

He made his way up the staircase and down the hall to Samantha's room. "Samantha?" He peeked inside the first bedroom on the left and saw the green dress laid out on the bed. He went inside.

As he waited, he glanced around her room. It was small and cluttered and very warm. It held the treasures of a young girl. From the patch-work quilt covering her bed to an assortment of books that lined the single bookshelf.

As he perused the space, his gaze fell on the stack of tabloids. *"Fifteen Magazine."* A photo of his younger self was splayed across the cover. He'd spent a large portion of his youth highlighted between their pages.

Curious, he picked it up to find the magazine underneath also depicted his smiling face. He grabbed the rest and flipped through them. His face stared up from the cover on each one.

As he made his way through the stack, he took note of the dates of publication. Most were from his mid to late teen years. Only a few were more recent. There was an older one about the charity he and his father had started. He turned to the page and scanned the article, finding details he'd almost forgotten.

While he held the magazine, he spotted a poster loosely rolled and propped in the corner. He unfurled it to see his own, much younger face, staring back at him.

A small noise came from behind and he turned. Samantha stood in the doorway holding two empty cardboard boxes. The wide-eyed and anguished expression on her face slammed his midsection.

"I take it this is the reading material you often spoke of."

An adorable flush peppered her cheeks. She opened her mouth to speak, thought better of it and clamped it shut.

"I have to say, I wouldn't have taken you for a reader of gossip rags." He suppressed a smile.

"Blake refers to them as gutter press."

"Smart man."

She raised her chin and pinned him with a cool stare. "A plain girl has to do something to entertain herself on Friday nights."

Choosing to ignore that, he nodded to the tabloid in his hand. "I had almost forgotten who I used to be. You reminded me, and for that I'm truly thankful." He tossed the magazine aside. "Looks like you've known me for quite some time."

"Yeah, me and a million other girls."

"There's that wall again," he said, as he stepped toward her. "So much is now clear. Your disdain for the adult me, your knowledge of my country, my father's charity and my part in it all those years ago."

Raw hurt glittered in her eyes. She swallowed and clutched the boxes to her chest like a shield.

"What are you doing here?" she asked.

He retrieved the boxes from her fingers and set them on the floor. "I'd like to explain about what Pricilla said to you."

"It doesn't matter."

"It does. Because it hurt you. When I said those words, I was throwing her taunt back into her face."

She folded her arms and leveled him with her Nanny Jane look.

He shook his head. "And if you think you can deter me with that Nanny Jane look, you're mistaken."

"Who?"

He'd have to tell her about Nanny Jane someday, but right now he just wanted her in his arms.

"I admit. I did use you, at first. I was so focused on me and my situation that I didn't think of how it might affect you. But as I spent time with you, got to know you, my plans changed where you were concerned."

"What plans?"

"Plans to make you mine." He took her hands in his. "I'm crazy in love with you, Samantha." He glanced at the magazines and the poster. "And I'm hoping the evidence suggests you might feel the same?"

Her eyes glistened with unshed tears. "Evidence of a stupid schoolgirl crush, you mean."

"Evidence that you are *the* most adorable creature I've ever known." He reached into his pocket and pulled out the ring. "Samantha Keller, my dearest and most beautiful swan, would you please accept this ring along with my heart?"

She swiped at a tear as a slow smile parted her lips. "What about your mother?"

"She basically told me I was a fool if I let someone of your caliber walk out of my life."

"Really?" Her tears turned to glistening jewels as her smile grew.

"Really."

"Well, if your mother likes me..." A mischievous twinkle filled her eyes. "Then... Yes."

He took hold of her hand and slid the ring on her finger. He held his breath and watched as she stood staring at her left hand. When she finally turned her gaze to his, she bubbled with laughter and threw her arms tightly around his neck.

He held her securely against his chest, exulting in the moment.

"I swear I think I've loved you all of my life," she said, burying her face in his neck.

He put her from him and cradled her face with his hands. "I so love hearing that."

He lifted his hand and plucked the clip from the

back of her head, releasing the severe bun. Her hair tumbled in a cascade of gold and brown around her shoulders. "You're a swan, Samantha. Don't you ever forget it."

He took her hand, sat on her bed, and pulled her down beside him. "I have something more to tell you. I have an architectural firm. I bet you haven't read about that."

"No." She shook her head.

"We save houses. Many of them Victorian. When I found out your home had gone into foreclosure, I had my lawyers set in motion the purchase of your home."

"What? That was you?"

"Yes."

"Why?"

"Well, after we're married, I'm assuming you'll be living with me in Sterlyn, and since you won't need this place, I thought it would be a nice home for the residents of Oakland Manor."

"Oh Marcus, that's wonderful. When did you do all of this?"

"Remember the day we had to leave Hudson early?"

She nodded.

"I had to sign the papers right away because another firm came in with an offer to buy it. No way was I going to let that happen."

She threw her arms around him, and he caught her close.

"Let's tell them tomorrow, when I return Miss Ellie's dress. It'll be a wonderful Christmas surprise."

CHAPTER 26

Samantha stood next to the sleek limousine parked outside The Carlyle Hotel. Queen Beatrice hugged her son goodbye, then turned to Sam.

"I haven't had this much fun in a long, long time." She clasped Sam's right hand. "I look forward to having you at the palace. We have a wedding to plan."

"Yes, ma'am, we do. And I look forward to it, as well."

Sam entwined her fingers with Marcus' and watched the limo pull away. "I keep thinking I'm going to wake up."

"Believe it or not, I feel the same way." His face creased into a smile.

"Let's go to the manor," she said. "I told Caroline I would spend Christmas with them. I can't wait to tell them the news."

The residents were in the midst of the day's celebration when Sam and Marcus arrived. After they joined them in the parlor, Sam passed out her gifts.

Their happiness in receiving the presents warmed her heart. It saddened her to think they weren't with their families, but then again, she wasn't either. At least they had each other.

As she watched their merriment, she found herself glancing at the stairway wondering if Miss Ellie would ever come down.

"You expecting someone?" Marcus asked.

"I was wondering why Miss Ellie hasn't joined us."

"Let's make the announcement, then we'll go check on her," he said.

Sam stood and got everyone's attention. "My dear Oakland Manor residents, Marcus and I are thrilled to inform you that we've found you a new home."

Their faces lit up like eager children expecting a treat.

"Marcus has purchased my house here in Queens. It's only a few blocks from here, so you'll still be in the same neighborhood."

"That's wonderful news," Caroline said, clapping her hands together. "I've been so worried about finding a place."

"Well, you can now relax," Marcus said. "I've worked out a schedule with a local contractor, and it looks like Samantha's house will be ready for you at the end of January."

Caroline stood and hugged Sam, then the other residents joined in. When the excitement died down, Miss

Clara offered seconds on coffee and pie, while Theo put the TV on one of the college football bowl games.

Sam took this time to give Marcus his gift.

He untied the knot from the festive gold ribbon and tore the paper away. "Victorian Houses of Hudson, New York. I love it. Thank you, Samantha."

He reached into his pocket and pulled out a small wrapped package. "For you."

A warm glow flowed through her as she took the gift and unwrapped it.

"Oh Marcus. This is lovely." The silver star ornament glistened as she held it up in the air. "Thank you. But you shouldn't have." She tenderly touched the sapphire on her left hand. "This ring is gift enough."

"The star is not what I originally wanted to give you. I'd gone back to purchase the crystal angel you'd admired in Hudson, but someone had already bought it."

"It's okay." She placed her hand to his left cheek. "It's the thought that counts."

"I suppose."

"Caroline, I have a present for Miss Ellie, and I need to return her dress. But she hasn't come downstairs this entire time."

"I'm sorry, who?"

"Miss Ellie. The lady who lives in the apartment at the top of the stairs."

Caroline frowned and ran a finger across her chin. "Sam, we don't have a Miss Ellie here."

"Elenore Terry."

"I'm sorry, but you're mistaken."

Sam blinked and stared, then turned to Marcus.

"On the contrary. Both Samantha and I have spoken to her." Marcus pointed to the top of the stairs. "Right up there."

"She lives on the third floor, in the attic apartment," Sam said.

"I know the room you're referring to. It's locked and no one has been in there for years."

Sam and Marcus wasted no time in heading for the staircase.

"Wait, you'll need the key," Caroline said.

They stood at the door of the apartment and knocked.

"Miss Ellie, It's Sam and Marcus," Sam said.

They eyed each other and waited for the door to open. Sam knocked again. "I have your dress."

"Here, I have the key." Caroline joined them, unlocked the door, and stepped aside for Marcus and Sam to enter.

The room was cold and sat in complete darkness. A damp, musty odor filled Sam's nostrils. Gone were the aromas of sweet cakes and tea. She fumbled for the light switch, found it, then turned it on. A single bulb cast a yellowish glare over the attic room. There was nothing at all familiar about the space. No twinkle lights, no tea kettle on the stove, and no fire in the grate.

"As you can see, no one has lived here for many years."

Sam took a few steps into the room, batting away cobwebs. "This is impossible." She swung around to face Caroline. "I'm telling you a sweet little woman has been living here." Sam threw her arm over the space. "Both of us sat in this room and had caramel cake with her."

"It's true, Caroline," Marcus said.

Sam marched to the mantel and ran her fingers over the wood, then held up her hand. Thick dust caked her fingertips.

"She used to be an actress and a costume maker. She...she worked on Broadway, for crying out loud. There were photos of her and her friends here on the mantel."

"And there was an Emmy Award," Marcus said.

"Yes, that, too."

"I don't know what to say." Caroline shrugged, thought a moment then smiled. "Maybe she was an angel. It is Christmas, after all," she said with a smile. "I'd better check on the residents. Maybe you can find an answer in one of these boxes. Lock up when you're done." Caroline handed Marcus the key and left.

Marcus pocketed the key and began helping in the search.

For the next few minutes, Sam and Marcus rummaged through the various cardboard boxes that were stacked in the middle of the room.

"Here's the Emmy." He held it up and read the inscription. "Elenore Terry, Best Costume Design, 1948, *Cinderella*."

"Elenore Terry. That's how she introduced herself to me. Then she told me everyone called her Ellie."

"Maybe there are two Elenore Terrys. Maybe our Miss Ellie is her descendant?"

Sam continued her search and found a bunch of framed pictures. "Marcus, aren't these the photos she had displayed on the mantel?"

He stepped to her side. "I have to confess I didn't pay much attention to them."

"Here's one where an actress is presenting the Emmy to... Miss Ellie. But she looks exactly the same in that seventy-year-old photo as she did last night." Sam's body tingled from head to toe. "How is this possible?" She checked the back of the frame, then held it up for him to see.

"Nineteen forty-eight." Marcus read the date, slowly, with a look on his face that told Sam he was as dumbfounded as her.

Sam turned her attention back to the photograph. "So. The person in this picture and Miss Ellie are one and the same."

"I believe so."

Sam shook her head as if her physical action of denial could somehow erase the miracle before them.

"Marcus, she knew about the promise I'd made to you."

"What promise?"

"Helping rid you of Pricilla."

"How in the world?"

"She said you came to see her—that you told her."

"I did no such thing. I've only been here once, with you."

"The night before last, after I'd heard Pricilla and Tiffany talking, I was upset, and I ran outside. I swear, she appeared out of nowhere. As if she'd been watching me."

They locked gazes as if waiting for the other to say what they were both thinking.

"It sounds to me like she was watching *over* you."

A small wrapped package sitting on the coffee table caught Sam's eye. "What's that?"

"It looks like a present." Marcus stepped over to the dusty table.

"But where did it come from?"

"I don't know." He picked it up and read the gift tag. The corners of his mouth lifted into a smile. "It's for you."

She took the present from his hand and read the tag.

For Samantha, a keepsake for our time together.

"It's not signed," she said.

"Maybe the gift will reveal the giver."

She clamped her lower lip with her teeth and peeled back the silver paper. Her breath caught. "Oh. My. Gosh." Sam held up the crystal angel.

"Is that the same—?"

"Yes. It's the one from the shop in Hudson."

Sam lifted her gaze to his, choking back tears. "Oh Marcus." Her tears fell, without reservation. "Miss Ellie was an angel."

"Not just any angel, your guardian angel." Marcus pulled her into his arms. "For God to have sent such a special messenger into your life is an honor, rarely given."

She sniffed and pulled out of his embrace. "If I could only thank her."

"She knows."

She nodded toward the photograph. "Seventy years. She must have been helping someone then too."

"An actress, maybe."

"I guess we'll never know." She gazed at the crystal angel in her hand. "I think I'll call her Miss Ellie."

He chuckled. "Completely appropriate."

She wound her arms around his neck. "So formal. Even now, surrounded by all of this magic."

"A lovely sentiment, then."

"Still too formal."

He hitched her closer. "You, my dear Miss Keller, are quite aggravating."

She lifted her left hand and wiggled her ring finger. "You'd better get used to it."

"How did I get so lucky?"

She glanced at the angel. "I'm not sure luck had anything to do with it."

He smiled and nodded. "Luck or not, you rock my world, Samantha. Because of you, I'm a better prince, and more importantly, a better man."

"And I'm the poster child that dreams really do come true."

Oblivious to the dust-laden room and the cobwebs surrounding them, Sam lifted her face to her beloved prince. And just as a sparkly angelic essence twirled and zipped toward the heavens, the prince lowered his mouth to hers with a kiss that held the promise of magic and wonder for as long as they both would live.

Thank you for reading!

Dear Reader,

I hope you enjoyed **The Princes Fake Fiancée**. I had so much fun writing Samantha and Prince Marcus' story!

I need to ask a favor. As you probably know, reviews can be hard to come by. And as a reader your feedback is so important. If you're so inclined, I'd love an honest review of *The Princes Fake Fiancée.* It doesn't have to be long or fancy. :) One or two sentences is fine.

If you have time, here's a link to my author page on Amazon. You can check out all my books here: http://www.amazon.com/-/e/B0077AG3ZM

In gratitude,

Darcy Flynn

About the Author

Award-Winning Author Darcy Flynn, is known for her heartwarming, sweet contemporary romances. Her refreshing storylines, irritatingly handsome heroes and feisty heroines will delight and entertain you from the first page to the last. Miss Flynn's heroes and heroines have a tangible chemistry that is entertaining, humorous and competitive.

Darcy lives with her husband and a menagerie of other living creatures on her horse farm in Franklin, Tennessee. She stargazes on warm summer nights and occasionally indulges in afternoon tea.

Although, published in the Christian non-fiction market under her real name, Joy Griffin Dent, it was the empty nest that turned her to writing romantic fiction. Proving that it's never too late to follow your dreams.

Please follow Darcy on Instagram:
Joydarcyauthor

Twitter:
@darcyflynn

and Facebook:
http:/www.facebook.com/DarcyFlynnAuthor

and visit her website: darcyflynnromances.com
or feel free to drop her a line at:
darcyflynnromances@gmail.com.

OTHER TITLES BY DARCY FLYNN:

Sealed With a Kiss – Prequel to Keeper of My Heart

Keeper of My Heart

Rogue's Son

Hawke's Nest – Like No Other Book 1

Eagle Eye – Like No Other Book 2

Double Trouble

Seven Days in December

Stowaway

CPSIA information can be obtained
at www.ICGtesting.com
Printed in the USA
LVHW041445281122
734169LV00016B/970